© 1994 NBAP

The Official Book

WRITTEN BY DOUG SMITH

To Raptors Fans and Friends Everywhere:

As a 15 year old, I dreamed of being involved with NBA basketball in my hometown – Toronto. With the support of my family and business partners, that dream has become a reality. It now encompasses all of the people who form the Raptors family, and more importantly, all of you. Without the assistance of Canadian basketball fans, this dream would have remained just another teenage memory.

Toronto Raptors: The Official Book tells the story of how the dream came to life: the people who got us there, and the events leading up to our inaugural season in the NBA. There were times when we weren't sure this day would ever come, but through it our enthusiasm remained high and there was never a dull moment. This book chronicles those moments with the hope that you will share with us the excitement that is the Toronto Raptors.

John Bitove

JOHN I. BITOVE (JR.)
President
Toronto Raptors Basketball Club Inc.

P.S. To J.J., Brett and Blair who missed their dad for two years.

A WHITECAP / OPUS BOOK

Published and produced by Opus Productions Inc.
300 West Hastings Street, Vancouver, British Columbia, Canada V6B 1K6

This edition published in Canada by Whitecap Books (Toronto) Limited, 602 Richmond Street West, Toronto, Ontario, Canada M5V 1Y9
Tel: (416) 703-0929

First Published in 1995

10 9 8 7 6 5 4 3 2 1

Canadian Cataloguing in Publication Data
Smith, Douglas G., 1958-
        Toronto Raptors

        ISBN 1-55110-389-3

        1. Toronto Raptors (Basketball team) I. Title
GV885.52.T67S64 1995   796.323'64'09713541   C95-911066-6

Printed and bound in Canada
by DW Friesen Ltd.

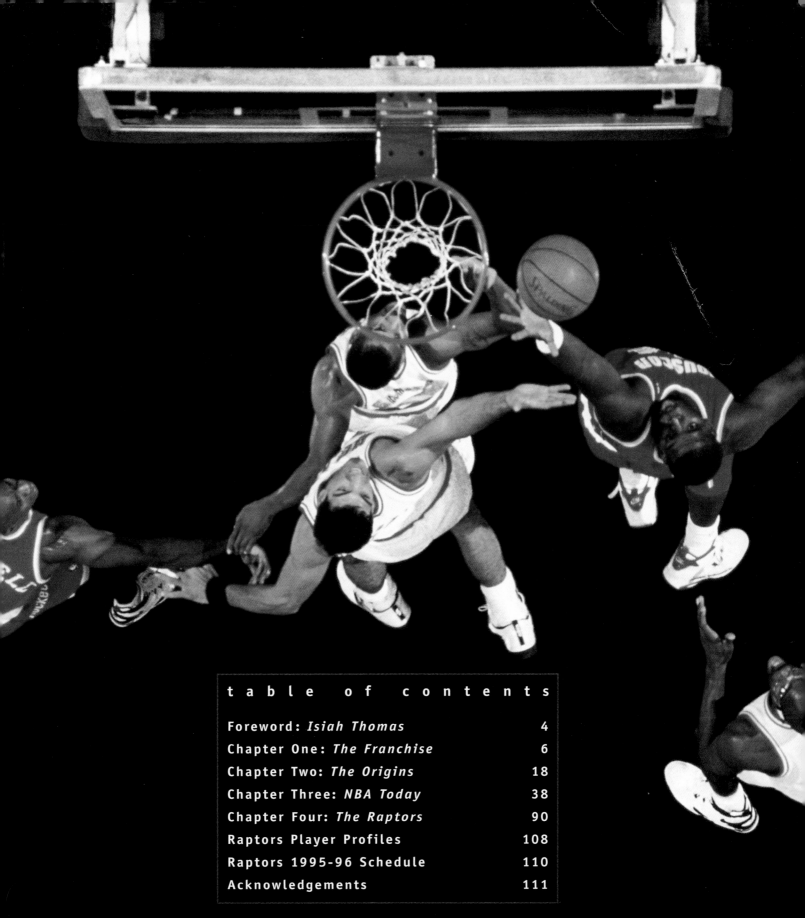

table of contents

An historic moment is upon us now as the Toronto Raptors take the court as the first international expansion team the NBA has ever had.

As we begin this momentous season, cheered on by hundreds of thousands of fans in Toronto, across Ontario and all of Canada, we are starting a process that we expect will take us someday to the pinnacle of professional basketball – an NBA championship.

The players who wear our Raptors uniforms in this, our first season, and in the future have been chosen for much more than just their basketball abilities. A true team is like a family; its members have to believe in the final goal and must be willing to work toward that goal every day. As with any family there may be squabbles, and tensions may develop, but, like any true family, we all know each of us is there to support one another.

We will go to any lengths in our efforts to try to find the winning formula for the Raptors. We will borrow ideas from the successful franchises in basketball and any other sport that we think can offer us insight into the development of a championship team.

One of the good things about our situation is that the people in Toronto are familiar with the expansion process thanks to the Blue Jays. I think everybody is familiar with the ups and downs they went through as an organization, yet they made it to the top and became world champions.

We will develop a Raptors way of doing things, an honourable way, a way that demonstrates our commitment to building a championship team and becoming a championship member of the community. We know we are more than just a basketball team, and we are committed to meeting and exceeding the expectations of the people of Toronto, of Ontario and of Canada at any moment.

When I retired from the Pistons a year and a half ago, I was looking for an opportunity in the game where I could really put my mark on a franchise. In Toronto, with the commitment I have from the other owners and the commitment I sense from our fans, that opportunity has presented itself. I welcome the challenge.

I was involved in helping the Pistons build their team and was lucky enough to have people like Jack McCloskey and Bill Davidson be so open with me in that regard. As the president of the NBA Players' Association, I was able to see that side of the game as well. I have a well-rounded view of the NBA and look forward to putting what I've learned into practice here.

Growing up in Chicago, I had many decisions to make that would forever alter my life's direction. I feel like I made the right decisions at every turn and I trust my judgment to make the right decisions now as the Vice President of Basketball Operations for the Toronto Raptors.

I look forward to this historic season, and I look forward to our first championship.

ISIAH THOMAS
Executive Vice President, Basketball Operations
Toronto Raptors Basketball Club Inc.

T H E

above: *Toronto Raptors have captured fans' imaginations with their dynamic logo, and have added their new team colours to the NBA rainbow.*

The night of September 30, 1993, was

going to be special for John Bitove, Jr.

After working day and night for months

F R A N C H I S E

on the biggest deal of his life, the

evening held the promise of a quiet

dinner with his wife, Randi, to celebrate

his 33rd birthday. His favourite table

at Gretzky's, a popular Toronto eatery

owned by the Bitove family, awaited.

facing page: *The man who brought the NBA north: The ability of John Bitove, Jr. to win the confidence of NBA owners and head office management led to the awarding of the NBA's historic first international franchise to Toronto.* left: *In 1992 the Miami Heat became the first of the last four expansion teams to make the playoffs, in their fourth season in the NBA.*

And then, shortly after 6 p.m., the telephone rang at the Bitove family home.

The subsequent conversation would forever alter John Bitove's life. Russ Granik, the deputy commissioner of the National Basketball Association, was at the other end of the line, and he wasn't calling to offer his birthday wishes. He had the big news Bitove had been waiting anxiously to hear. Earlier that day, the league's expansion committee had unanimously decided to grant the group led by Bitove the right to own the league's first international franchise. The quiet birthday dinner would become a double celebration. Not only had another year passed, but Bitove had realized one of the biggest dreams of his life. He will have many other birthdays, but calls like Granik's come once in a lifetime.

"I felt satisfaction more than joy," Bitove recalls of his immediate reaction. "Satisfaction that all our hard work had paid off. I remember saying to my wife, 'Let's enjoy tonight because it's going to be crazy for the next few years.' I made sure we had fun 'til three or four in the morning that night because there was a lot of work to do right away."

As understatements go, that one's as big as Shaquille O'Neal.

The NBA is on the cutting edge of professional sports worldwide. The NBA ownership circle is a select group, one that many others would give anything to join. When Bitove got that fateful call, it culminated years of work behind the scenes, including a very public battle with two other Toronto groups, and set in motion a business plan that entails expenditures of more than a quarter of a billion dollars. It also meant Toronto would have its own NBA franchise, finishing a process that had begun almost a decade before.

The NBA grants expansion franchises only after close scrutiny of the bidding groups, and only when it makes sense for the league. The last time it admitted new members was in 1987.

The decision to add Charlotte, Miami, Orlando and Minnesota made perfect sense at the time. The NBA wanted a presence in the fastest-growing state in the Union, hence the Florida franchises. Charlotte was the centre of the biggest hotbed of basketball not served by a professional league. Minnesota had once been home to the Lakers, who represented the first dynasty in the fledgling league, so there were sentimental reasons for awarding that franchise.

top: *On October 18, 1992, Bitove was given the chance to stage the 1994 World Championship of Basketball. Three days later, bidding for the Toronto franchise began.* bottom: *Dreams of glory: Toronto had its first taste of world-class basketball when it hosted the 1994 World Championship of Basketball. Isiah Thomas (pictured here, bottom row, far left), selected to the 1994 Dream Team (though he did not play due to injury), experienced first hand how well his new home responded to NBA calibre play.*

left: *The Bitove group's splendid success in mounting the championship helped convince NBA powers they would be an exemplary choice to own the Toronto franchise.*

At the time, Toronto had entered a bid, which galvanized the city and first turned it on to the possibility of having a team of its own. Concert magnates Bill Ballard and Michael Cohl, along with partner Robert Cohl and financiers Paul and David Fingold, had enlisted the aid of none other than basketball legend Wilt Chamberlain to help tug at the heartstrings of the NBA decision makers. They had everything, it appeared, except timing. The NBA wanted to satisfy domestic markets, so Toronto's bid didn't qualify. However, the NBA's interest in Toronto had been whetted, and the right time for NBA basketball to come to Canada would soon be around the corner.

Recalls NBA Commissioner David Stern: "You can't help but notice that Toronto is one of the great North American cultural and business and sports centres, and Vancouver is an extraordinary city that has become a jumping-off point for Asia. So for us, watching major league baseball and hockey, we became very much aware of those two cities."

It was in 1990 that Bitove first considered the possibility of mounting his own bid to bring the NBA to Toronto. A graduate of Indiana University, he had seen and lived with some of the most avid basketball fans on the earth. He dreamed of the day when the game would come to his hometown. So he started meeting with NBA officials whenever the opportunity arose. When he bid for and won the right to stage the 1994 World Championship of Basketball, he enlisted the aid of the NBA marketing wizards to help him promote the event. In this way, he became a familiar face to the movers and shakers of the league, all the while biding his time until expansion fever next hit and he could strike. He waited patiently, quietly in the wings, for the right moment.

And then his hand was forced.

A Toronto group led by construction magnate Larry Tanenbaum made a pre-emptive strike in the expansion lottery by sending a $100,000 deposit cheque to the league's head office early in 1993. The Tanenbaum group, which would come to include two heavy hitters in Labatt Breweries and the Canadian Imperial Bank of Commerce, sent the money unsolicited, but their actions made the league sit up and it accelerated the expansion process. Labatt and the CIBC were the prime movers behind the extraordinarily successful Toronto Blue Jays, so their involvement was impressive from a business and marketing standpoint.

left: *Proud culmination to heroic effort: The quietly exultant Bitove partnership announces it has won the right to Canada's first NBA franchise. Pictured (back row, from left) Borden Osmak, David Coriat, Isiah Thomas, John Bitove, Gary Slaight (front row, from left) Allan Slaight, David Peterson, Phil Granovsky.*

All this simply made Bitove work harder. He went about attracting the solid businessmen he knew would impress the NBA expansion committee and picked people who possessed particular skills. He called on broadcasting executive Allan Slaight, whose expertise would prove invaluable; and on former Ontario premier David Peterson, whose political savvy cannot be dismissed. He brought in Borden Osmak and the Bank of Nova Scotia, as well as family friend Phil Granovsky.

At the end of the day, Bitove had put together a powerful, influential and, above all, dedicated collection of partners.

"When I was putting the group together, money was no object because everyone wanted to be part of this thing," recalls Bitove. "We wanted to put together a group where everyone who came to the table had something to offer that was more than money. I think the group we ended up with gives us expertise in every imaginable area we'll need."

The process became even more complicated with the addition of a Ballard-Cohl group back for a second kick at the can, promising an arena on the site of the Canadian National Exhibition. The group went on the offensive early and became a public favourite when it brought on board Magic Johnson to help cement its case. Johnson, retired from the NBA but still inexorably linked to the sport and loved by its fans, called a news conference in Toronto at which he vowed to do everything in his power to help his new partners.

Bitove knew just his familiarity with league officials would not be enough, so his group did what it had to in order to impress the expansion committee and the league office with a solid business plan and a willingness to work with the other owners around the table. When the final decision came from the NBA office, they had won a huge battle, one few thought they could. According to Commissioner Stern, "There was a very comfortable level of interaction with the Bitove group."

One key piece was missing: the man who would shape the way the franchise played basketball as general manager and vice president responsible for basketball operations. John Bitove had two choices when filling the position. He could have recycled an experienced NBA executive, as many other teams have done, or he could take a bold step with a new face. It had never been a secret that Isiah Thomas aspired to something more than retiring from the game to a life of luxury, and when his name came across Bitove's desk, alarms went off.

Thomas was, like Bitove, a graduate of Indiana University, and as a fervent basketball fan Bitove used to cheer Thomas on during his Hoosier days.

"In terms of the younger candidates we had, Isiah was it, no question," says Bitove. "His ideas were very progressive on how the sport should and would change on the basketball management side of things, and he was a perfect fit for what we were trying to do as a franchise."

Thomas has been making an impression on people since he left Chicago to start his college career. With the Hoosiers, the gifted point guard led his team to a national championship before leaving, after his sophomore year, for the NBA. He was drafted by a struggling Detroit Pistons team, but the franchise's future looked bright from the day he signed on in 1981. With Thomas at the helm, the Pistons won NBA titles in 1989 and 1990. He earned a reputation as one of the most intense competitors in the league, striving to win at practically all costs. It is this level of commitment that he brings to his new job. He also brings a familiar face along to help him construct his first team. Brendan Malone, an assistant coach with the Pistons from 1986-95, impressed Thomas enough during his tenure in Detroit, and again during a free-agent camp the Raptors held in Toronto in May 1995, to be hired as the team's first coach.

When Thomas is in the room with Bitove and the partners, he's more than just a high-level employee. He has a 4½ percent ownership stake in the team, a testament to his desire to be more than just the basketball guy. "There were a few things I was looking for," Thomas recalls. "I wanted a major role in an organization; I wanted to own part of the team; I was willing to put up my own money; and I wanted a city that would embrace the type of feeling I wanted to bring and Toronto offered all of that."

The Raptors have succeeded in many of the important areas for any first-year sporting franchise. Choosing a name and developing a personality, selling tickets to games for a team before it even exists and enlisting the aid of key corporate sponsors have been accomplished in spectacular terms. Already the Raptors are at the league's highest level of sponsorship revenue.

facing page: *A pivotal element in the Detroit Pistons' resurgence in the 1980s, Isiah Thomas shared in winning two consecutive NBA titles.*
right: *Thomas' experience with Brendan Malone during his days with the Pistons, helped persuade him that Malone had the strength of character to be head coach of a fledgling expansion team.*
far right: *Public introduction of Isiah Thomas as the Raptors' general manager and vice president responsible for basketball operations was staged with a flourish.*

left: *Destined to be a showplace for the 21st century, the 22,500-seat Air Canada Centre will be home to the Raptors in their third season. Its design, by Brisbin Brook Beynon, Architects of Toronto and HOK of Kansas City, incorporates the unique stone carvings and facade of the existing building into a futuristic steel, glass and concrete structure. The first chapter of the Raptors' NBA story will unfold in the nearby SkyDome.*
facing page: *The NBA's best will be thrilling Canadian fans, and pictured here are two of the league's brightest luminaries: Michael Jordan and Shaquille O'Neal.*

Merchandise took off like a rocket as the team quickly vaulted into the top 10 sellers worldwide among the NBA franchises. The Raptors logo is identifiable coast-to-coast, which has given the franchise an in with the populace even before a player laces up a sneaker.

The ticket-selling campaign was a difficult task, given the NBA's insistence on at least 12,500 season-tickets sold by December 31, 1994. In an overwhelming display of enthusiasm, the team went over the 15,000 mark a few days before Christmas, ahead of the league deadline by over a week. It marked a watershed moment in franchise history and proved to Bitove once and for all that the Toronto market would support an NBA team.

The ticket campaign and merchandising success have also convinced the corporate sector to jump on board. The new 22,500-seat arena, to be named the Air Canada Centre, is one of the biggest deals Bitove has made.

While adults will represent the largest group of ticket buyers in the first few years of the franchise's existence, any sustained growth in the Raptors' fan base will have to come from today's teenagers – hard-core young fans who have grown up during the NBA's heyday.

Today's kids relate to the game and its players on a level that far exceeds their interest in any other sport. Where kids of an earlier era grew up idolizing hockey players and could dissect skill levels of players like seasoned observers, teens today know who has the best jump shot, the best move to the basket or plays the best defence in the NBA.

This bodes well for the Raptors as they look down the road for their fan base of the future.

It has all added up to prove what Bitove thought when he set the wheels in motion. The NBA is the best sports league to join at this juncture in history, and membership in it opens a myriad of possibilities.

THE

above: *Abundant harvest: From humble beginnings, the sport of basketball has grown to world stature. Peach baskets served as goals for the first game.*
facing page: *Dr. James A. Naismith, 1861-1939, the inventor of the game.*

A goalkeeper, two guards, three centre men and two wings took their places

O R I G I N S

on the hardwood floor at the Young Men's Christian Association gymnasium in Springfield, Massachusetts, on a December day in 1891, facing a like number of contemporaries deployed on the other side of the gym's centre line.

Basketball's birthplace: The YMCA Training School gymnasium, Springfield, Massachusetts, circa 1891.

Dressed in long-sleeved jerseys and long grey trousers, they were about to indulge their instructor in his attempt to devise some type of recreational activity for the winter months that didn't involve the rough-house tactics of rugby or lacrosse, two sports the instructor knew intimately, but two he also realized didn't translate well to the indoor forum.

Around the room was suspended a balcony for spectators that also doubled as a running track for men trying to keep up their physical fitness. It was a dimly lit gym, about 45 feet wide and 65 feet long. The playing surface, marked out not with painted lines but with clubs, dumbbells and the other trappings of a gymnastics class of the era, measured somewhere in the neighbourhood of 35 by 50 feet.

Suspended from the balconies at either end, thanks to the quick thinking of "Pop" Stebbins, the YMCA's janitor known for his packrat tendencies, were two peach baskets, their 15-inch diameter openings tapered to about eight inches at the bottom. The ball was an Association football, the type used for many other games and chosen for this new endeavour simply by

chance. The seemingly simple object of the game was to get the ball into the opponents' basket.

With Stebbins standing by with a step-ladder to retrieve balls that might nestle in the bottom of the peach baskets – only later were the bottoms cut out – the boys played for about 45 minutes, managing just once to get the ball in the basket. Nevertheless, that goal by William R. Chase from near the mid-point line (the first three-pointer?) set the wheels in motion.

The sporting spectrum would be forever changed from that December day forward, and the young instructor felt a sense of accomplishment when the class ended. It took a while for his newfangled game to gain universal acceptance, and the predictable growing pains at times made it appear as if it would not survive. But with that one toss of the ball, the one basket by William R. Chase and the decision to offer young men an alternative to the games they had known, the young YMCA instructor by the name of James A. Naismith had invented basketball. Little did he know, the game would turn into one of the most popular sports worldwide.

In the gently rolling hills of eastern Ontario lies the tiny town of Almonte, population about 4,400, and with the same look as countless other rural communities in countless other provinces and states.

From this sleepy Ontario town, James A. Naismith began an incredible life's journey that took him to Montreal, to Springfield, to Denver and to Kansas. Orphaned as a youngster when his parents died of typhoid, young Naismith moved to Almonte where he lived with an aunt and uncle. As a teen, he decided to dedicate his life to the ministry and enrolled in the Presbyterian College of McGill University in Montreal. As with many struggling young students, he had to find a way to make the money to pay for his education, so he took a job as a physical education instructor at a nearby gymnasium. Naismith saw a correlation between spiritual and physical fitness and enrolled in the School for Christian Workers in Springfield after his graduation from divinity school.

That School for Christian Workers soon became the Young Men's Christian Association Training School, and it was there

that Naismith, a 30-year-old temporary instructor of physical education, held that historic first game of basketball. While he initially developed the game as one of a more genteel nature than rugby or lacrosse, the bumps and bruises he saw set him on another path – to medical school in Denver where he added an MD degree to his rapidly growing list of accomplishments. Naismith finally settled at the University of Kansas, where he taught and helped refine such sports as fencing, golf, track, rowing and lacrosse. He served as the school's director of physical education until he was replaced by the legendary Forrest "Phog" Allen in the mid-1920s.

As one would expect from a divinity school graduate, YMCA instructor and college professor, Naismith was an altruistic sort who saw athletics in their purest and most simple of terms, keeping young men healthy of body and healthy of mind. But natural selection dictated that basketball would not remain a game played in tiny gyms in out-of-the-way locations. Basket-ball would evolve, and it was only a matter of time before it joined the ranks of the professional sporting world.

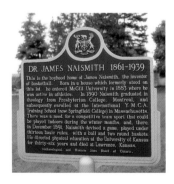

left: *In the countryside near Ottawa, on the outskirts of the quiet town of Almonte, sits an historic landmark plaque commemorating Naismith's childhood home. Inside the house, now a museum, memorabilia tells the story of the father of basketball and the origins of the game.*
facing page: *James A. Naismith lived to see the game he invented flourish to national popular appeal. Naismith is pictured here at the University of Kansas, where he was director of physical education.*

Circa 1910 basketball that was found above Naismith's office at the University of Kansas.

ORIGINAL RULES

The NBA rule book is a complex and sometimes confusing piece of legislation, governing such happenstance as shattered backboards, 24-second clocks, illegal defences, fights between players, uniform numbers and the colour of shoes.

James Naismith's first set of rules, set down in December 1891, were simple and to the point:

The ball is to be an ordinary Association foot ball.

1. The ball may be thrown in any direction with one or both hands.

2. The ball may be batted in any direction with one or both hands (never with the fist).

3. A player cannot run with the ball; the player must throw it from the spot on which he catches it; allowance to be made for a man who catches the ball when running at a good speed.

4. The ball must be held in or between the hands; the arms or body must not be used for holding it.

5. No shouldering, holding, pushing, tripping or striking in any way the person of an opponent shall count as a foul. The first infringement of this rule by any person shall count as a foul, the second shall disqualify him until the next goal is made, or if there was evident intent to injure the person, for the whole of the game, no substitution allowed.

6. A foul is striking at the ball with the fist, violation of Rules 3 and 4, and such as described in Rule 5.

7. If either side makes three consecutive fouls, it shall count as a goal for the opponents (consecutive means without the opponents in the meantime making a foul).

8. A goal shall be made when the ball is thrown or batted from the ground into the basket and stays there, providing those defending the goal do not touch or disturb the goal. If the ball rests on the edge and the opponent moves the basket, it shall count as a goal.

9. When the ball goes out of bounds it shall be thrown into the field and played by the person first touching it. In case of a dispute the umpire shall throw it straight into the field. The thrower in is allowed five seconds; if he holds it longer it shall go to the opponent. If any side persists in delaying the game, the umpire shall call a foul on them.

10. The umpire shall be judge of the men, and shall note the fouls, and notify the referee when three consecutive fouls have been made. He shall have the power to disqualify men according to Rule 5.

11. The referee shall be judge of the ball and shall decide when the ball is in play, in bounds, and to which side it belongs, and shall keep the time. He shall decide when a goal has been made, and keep account of the goals with any other duties that are usually performed by a referee.

12. The time shall be two fifteen minute halves, with five minutes rest between.

13. The side making the most goals in that time shall be declared winners. In case of a draw the game may, by agreement of the captains, be continued until another goal is made.

Franchises came and went, affiliations changed, so the best teams switched to barnstorming the cities of the East and the Midwest, playing challenge matches against local heroes. In the rough and tumble epoch between the wars, one team personified finesse: New York City's Original Celtics. Nat Holman (pictured), renowned for his passing ability and deceptive ball-handling manoeuvres, was a Celtic standout.

November 1, 1946, Toronto, Ontario, Maple Leaf Gardens: That night the crowds milled about outside, waiting to become part of history. The venerable hockey shrine, open for about 15 years, was going to play host to the first-ever game of the Basketball Association of America, pitting the Toronto Huskies against the New York Knickerbockers, and there was excitement in the air.

Basketball had come a long way since that day in Springfield. Barnstorming teams had criss-crossed the United States spreading the gospel. The college game had taken off; Madison Square Garden in New York was the mecca of the game, playing host to college doubleheaders that were the envy of basketball promoters everywhere. Still, the game was thought of as a college game. The professional leagues that sprung up regionally in the northeast and midwest of the country had not caught on.

But with the Second World War ending, tens of thousands of young men and women would need something to fill their leisure hours, and the owners of ice arenas and professional hockey teams needed something to help fill the seats and vacant dates. Thus was born the Basketball Association of America, led by the president of the American Hockey League, Maurice Podoloff, and tied tightly to the homes of hockey teams in cities such as Toronto, Pittsburgh, Cleveland, Boston and New York. Podoloff, a Canadian citizen, was the fledgling league's first president and later became the NBA's inaugural president.

In Toronto, curiosity ruled the day. Charles Watson, an official with Canadian Breweries Ltd., was the president of the team and had convinced industrialist H. S. Shannon, local stockbroker Eric Cradock and Ben Newman, a businessman from St. Catharines, Ontario, to take a chance on the new league. Realizing the game itself might be a tough sell, Watson persuaded one of the best known sports figures of the era, Lew Hayman, to come on board as general manager.

So all eyes were on the Gardens that evening. The game attracted 7,090 fans to the shrine of hockey who sat excitedly through the game New York eventually won 68-66. It was the beginning of what the Toronto owners hoped was a long association with the new league. This was not to be.

Ed Sadowski, signed away from Fort Wayne, Indiana, to a lucrative $10,000 contract to be the player/coach of the Huskies, quickly found out he wasn't cut out for both duties.

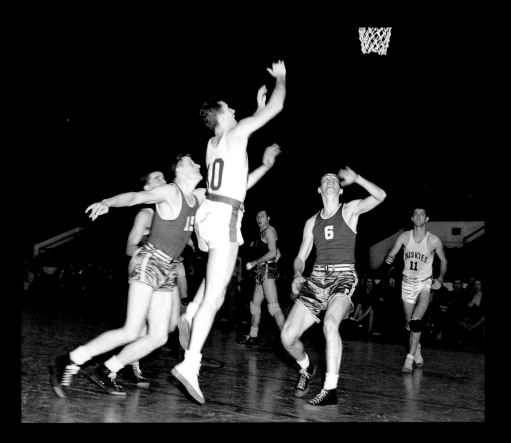

top: *The Basketball Association of America was the precursor to the NBA: Here, the Toronto Huskies and Pittsburgh Ironmen play at Maple Leaf Gardens in December 1946.* bottom: *Huskies' Dick Fitzgerald, left, and Clarence "Kleggie" Hermsen take a breather alongside coach Bob "Red" Rolfe.*

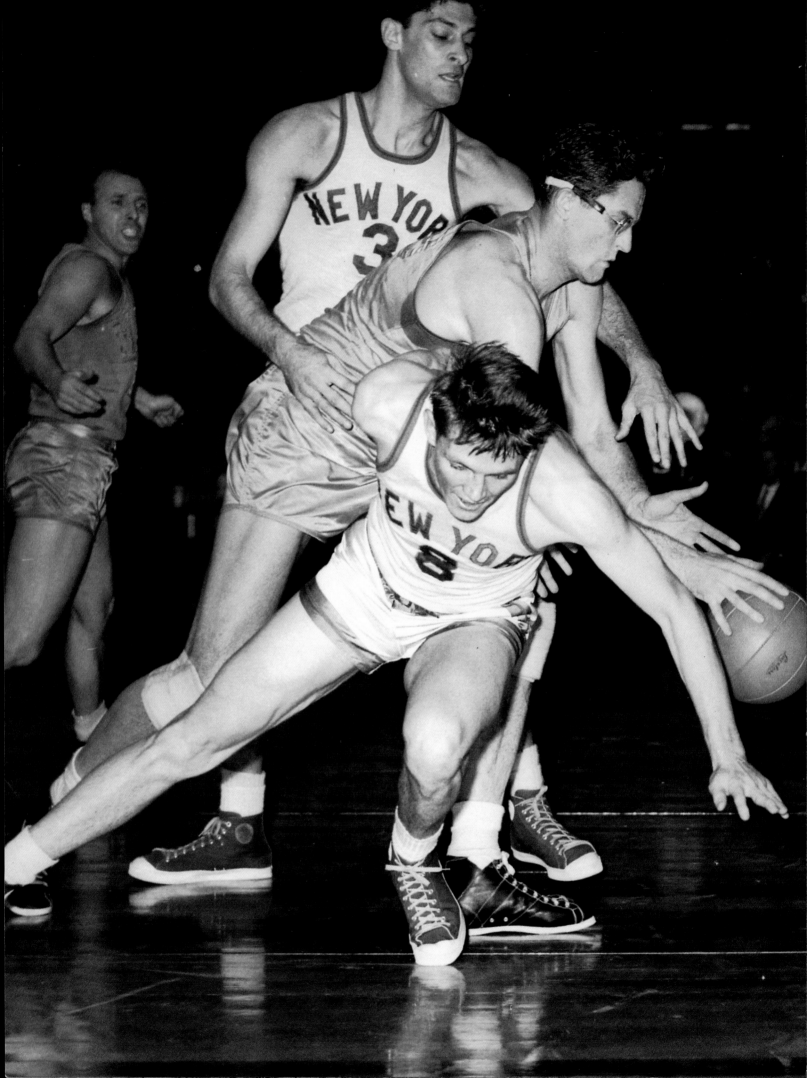

The team got off to a 3-8 start – hardly the way to attract new fans to a winter sport in the home of the Toronto Maple Leafs. Hayman had little choice but to try to persuade his high-priced athlete to give up his coaching duties and concentrate solely on playing, but Sadowski bolted from the team during a road trip to Providence, and the Huskies were sinking like a stone.

Hayman filled in as coach for one game – a loss – before turning over the helm to "Red" Rolfe, a starter with baseball's New York Yankees and a former basketball coach at Yale University. The Huskies continued to limp along, struggling home with a miserable 22-38 record, tied for dead last in the league's Eastern Division with the Boston Celtics. Attendance plummeted, the financial losses mounted, and the Basketball Association of America experiment north of the 49th parallel came to an end in June of 1947 when Hayman pulled the plug.

The growing pains of any new venture are harsh; those of a new professional sports league are that much harsher. After the first eventful season – Philadelphia beat Chicago four games to one to win the inaugural championship – the Basketball Association of America franchises in Toronto, Cleveland,

Pittsburgh and Detroit folded. By the time the 1949-50 season rolled around, the BAA had expanded and contracted, grown and shrunk and finally absorbed six franchises from the rival, Midwest-based National Basketball League. Wanting to come up with a fresh new look, name and image, the National Basketball Association was born.

There were 17 teams in the new league, from New York to Sheboygan, Denver to Washington, Boston to Minneapolis. George Mikan, the most talked about basketball player on earth at the time, a six-foot-10 giant who would revolutionize the game, was the league's marquee player. In what would become known as the Mikan Era, he led the Minneapolis Lakers to five championships between 1949 and 1954 and was literally and figuratively a towering figure in the world of sports. A brilliant player at Chicago's DePaul University, Mikan was able to bring to the NBA many of the fans who watched him throughout his college career, and he went on to be voted Mr. Basketball of the First Half Century for his play in college and in the pros. He was the first player to become synonymous with the league, but he certainly wasn't the last.

facing page: *Dominant BAA star George Mikan drives between two Knicks defenders during a 1948 game.*
right: *Mikan and fellow Minnesota Lakers visit the White House while in town for the final BAA championship series in 1949.*
far right: *Over a nine-year professional career Mikan averaged 21.5 points per game and 13.4 rebounds per game.*

There have been dynasties in every sport and every sporting era. The New York Yankees treated baseball's World Series like their own rite of autumn in the 1950s and 1960s; the Montreal Canadiens were perennial Stanley Cup champions in the same era. But few teams in any sport in any league in any country in the world can match the success of the Boston Celtics of the NBA. Playing in the magical and mystical Boston Garden – where leprechauns lived and general manager Red Auerbach made sure the opposition was treated with predictable hostility and cold water in the locker room – the Celtics of the Bill Russell era were unmatched in their success.

In 1956-57, in every season between 1958-59 and 1965-66 and again in 1967-68 and 1968-69, the Celtics were NBA champions. Russell, the six-foot-10 centre from the University of San Francisco, and Bob Cousy, the magician of the backcourt from Holy Cross, were the league's dominant duo. Cousy led the NBA in assists for eight straight seasons. Russell was the anchor of the frontcourt and was also the single greatest defender of his time, a brilliant shot-blocker who corralled 21,721 rebounds in his career. He won 11 NBA titles in 13 seasons, was the league's Most Valuable Player five times and appeared in 12 All-Star Games. For many fans, Russell and Cousy and the Celtics *were* the NBA.

Russell's perfect foil was his most bitter rival, Wilt Chamberlain. Where Russell was the dominant defender and a perennial member of a championship team, Chamberlain was the most gifted offensive performer of his era. Although he amassed 31,419 points in a 14-year career, Chamberlain won but two NBA titles: 1967 with the Philadelphia 76ers and 1972 with the Los Angeles Lakers. His teams lost to Russell and the Celtics in three other championship series.

There can be no denying Chamberlain's offensive prowess. On the night of March 2, 1962, playing for the Philadelphia Warriors against the New York Knickerbockers, the big man scored 100 points – an NBA record which has yet to be seriously challenged. He was 36 of 63 from the field, 28 of 32 from the free-throw line. That night, he scored 23 points in the first quarter, 18 in the second, 28 in the third and ended the incredible evening with a 31-point fourth quarter – the single greatest offensive output in NBA history.

To fully appreciate where the league is, it's wise to consider where it once was. There was a time in the not-too-distant past when the NBA didn't enjoy nearly the kind of fame, fortune and adulation it has today and was in danger of disappearing. In the early and mid-1970s, it was a league on the decline. Attendance was down, allegations of drug use by some players had created a negative public image, and there were serious concerns about the league's future. Television networks all but ignored the game as the league's championship series wasn't deemed popular or important enough to rate live network coverage.

But as the 1970s became the 1980s, those difficulties were solved. The drug problem was eradicated by a combination of enlightened leadership in the players union and forward-thinking, aggressive campaigns from the league office. The technological advances in telecommunications, so critical to today's game, came fast and furious, and the league's fortunes were altered permanently. It was like magic.

Or, rather, it was Magic.

To understand why the NBA is where it is today, why the 1990s have been so good, one has to look to the 1980s. And that examination has to start with the brilliant smile and gifted athleticism of Earvin "Magic" Johnson. More than any player in contemporary time, Johnson gave the NBA life. He redefined the playing of the game, doing in a six-foot-nine-inch frame what used to be the sole domain of the little man. He dribbled the ball with that grin lighting up arenas, he threw those picture-perfect no-look passes – always, it seemed, staring into a television camera when he flipped the ball over his shoulder. As a rookie in 1979-80, he took the Los Angeles Lakers to the NBA title, playing centre in the final game for the injured Kareem Abdul-Jabbar. His joy was palpable, his enthusiasm contagious, and he became synonymous with the fun that the NBA has now become.

Four more times in that decade – in 1982, 1985, 1987 and 1988 – he took his team to the top of the mountain. He helped make Lakers games "Showtime" for the Hollywood entertainment jetset. And, if the movie stars liked it and sat in the front rows for the games, it was only a matter of time before the general public took notice.

far left: *Magic Johnson shares a lighter moment with teammates on the bench.*
left: *With his stellar play and sparkling personality, Magic captivated fans throughout the 1980s, and inspired his Lakers to four NBA Championships.*
facing page: *Simply Magic: Throughout the 1980s, one player's name was synonymous with basketball for much of the world. Earvin "Magic" Johnson redefined the game as it is played from the guard position. Along the way, he inspired and delighted a new generation of NBA fans.*

facing page: *Johnson's talented nemesis, the understated Larry Bird led his Celtics to three championships. Each player won three league MVPs.*
far left: *Cool in demeanour, Larry Bird played with a passionate intensity within. His consuming desire to win and night-in, night-out effort set an example for his Celtics teammates to follow.*
left: *Less showy than his rival Johnson, Bird nonetheless earned recognition from those who know basketball. He followed up his Rookie-of-the-Year title in 1980 with three straight league MVP honours (1984 through 1986).*

But Johnson needed a rival who was his equal to bring out his very best. While he was working his magic in the make-believe world of Hollywood, his alter-ego was doing the same across the continent in Boston, where Larry Bird, the quiet young man from French Lick, Indiana, was enhancing the already-rich Celtic tradition. Johnson was gregarious, Bird more understated. Johnson was flashy, Bird workmanlike. Each man brought greatness to his team. Bird's team won NBA Championships in 1981, 1984 and 1986. Three times Bird and Johnson met in the NBA Finals. Twice the Lakers were victorious and once the Celtics ruled on the day.

The two men, so different in mannerism but so similar in skill, dedication and determination, were the perfect bookends to help establish the league. Johnson and Bird demonstrated that there were places in the pantheon of greats for men who played different styles of the game in contemporary times.

Johnson played at breakneck speed, getting out fast on the break, pounding the ball up the court at every opportunity. He was a giant among guards and teams were in a quandary about how to stop him. He was too tall for the normal guard to handle; he controlled the ball too well for a forward to defend. He showed fans, coaches and opponents that big men need not wait for the ball to come to them. He invented the big guard position, perfected it, and set the standard by which all others are measured.

At the other end of the court was Bird, not blessed with the natural athletic brilliance of Johnson, but no less a complete player. He had an uncanny knack for getting open for his patent jump shot, and he worked tirelessly every minute he was on the floor. Where Johnson changed the game, Bird showed there was still a place for guile and hard work as much as there was a place for speed and leaping ability.

As chroniclers of the game delve into the contributions of Julius Erving, Magic Johnson, Larry Bird, Isiah Thomas, Michael Jordan, Shaquille O'Neal, Hakeem Olajuwon and the rest of the more contemporary superstars, they cannot overlook the likes of George Mikan, Bob Cousy, Bill Russell, Wilt Chamberlain, Elgin Baylor, Oscar Robertson and Jerry West and the roles they played in bringing the game to prominence in the sporting universe.

following pages: *Legends in the making: A galaxy of superstars scramble for the ball during Game 6 of the 1987 NBA Finals. Lakers won the game to beat Celtics for the championship.*

above: *Sphere of influence: Today's fine-tuned Official NBA Basketball bears little resemblance to Naismith's original Association football.*

facing page: *Three-peat? Hoping to carry last season's glory into the next, 1995 Playoff MVP Hakeem Olajuwon, draped in Houston Rockets' new uniform, cradles his trophy.*

In a bygone era an aura of polite attentiveness carried the sporting day in arenas and stadiums throughout

T O D A Y

North America. There were no raucous antics, no celebrities in the front rows. Overwhelming importance was placed on the sport, and entertainment was left to the movie houses and theatres. That was then. And this is now.

far left: *Fans in Houston cheer on their Rockets during the 1995 NBA Finals.*
left: *Mexico City gets into the NBA spirit during an exhibition game. The NBA also plays exhibition games in Japan and Europe, taking its excitement to an international audience.*

The house lights dim as the performers prepare to take their places on the stage. The spotlights shine with white hot intensity and laser lights dance across the floor. The music – pulsating, modern, loud music – thunders out of dozens of mammoth speakers, exhorting the audience into a frenzy. At every break in the action, something happens. An acrobatic team here, a dance team there, a mascot playing to the crowd. A cornucopia of sights and sounds makes every night in the NBA a memorable one.

Welcome to the NBA, where sports and entertainment are linked at every level, and every game's a festival.

"Our teams have recognized a phenomenon of the 1990s – that fans want very much to be part of the experience," says NBA Commissioner David Stern. "They have really focused on the entire entertainment experience."

And no one does it better than the NBA.

In the contemporary world of professional sports leagues, the NBA has become the benchmark by which all others are measured. It has taken the entire sports industry to new levels. Its influence reaches far beyond the borders of its member cities and into nearly every country on the globe. Its era of growth has made basketball unquestionably The Game of the 1990s. The many reasons for its extraordinary success are varied and diverse.

"In our case, the owners and the teams and the league office and the television networks began work on a lot of different fronts, and they all seemed to come together," is how the commissioner explains the steady growth. "The boom in arenas, the boom in cable television and network television, the boom in sports league-identified merchandise, the boom in TV outside of the United States, the boom in technology through direct satellite broadcasts, CD-ROM, interactivity, the Internet. The growth in all those areas has been tremendously important in contributing to our growth."

Added to this is the attractiveness of the sport and its players. In the simplest of terms, basketball – NBA basketball – is the perfect game for its time. The court, 94 by 50 feet, is a perfect fit for television and allows the kind of closeups that give even the fan at home a sense of being involved in the action. The intensity of the action can be seen in the eyes of the players, up close and personal, which lends an intimacy to the game that exists in no other sport.

The dance teams in action. top: Houston's Rocket Power Dancers and Turbo, the team
mascot. bottom, left: One of Chicago's LuvaBulls. bottom, right: A member of

THE COLOURS OF THE NBA

ATLANTA HAWKS
Franchise history Joined NBA as Tri-Cities Blackhawks in 1949-50, became Milwaukee Hawks in 1951-52, became St. Louis Hawks in 1955-56, became Atlanta Hawks in 1968-69
NBA titles Won NBA Championship in St. Louis 1958
Ones to watch Stacey Augmon, Steve Smith, Mookie Blaylock

BOSTON CELTICS
Franchise history Charter member in 1946-47
NBA titles Won NBA Championships in 1957, 1959, 1960, 1961, 1962, 1963, 1964, 1965, 1966, 1968, 1969, 1974, 1976, 1981, 1984 and 1986
Ones to watch Dee Brown, Dino Radja, Dana Barros

CHARLOTTE HORNETS
Franchise history Began as expansion team in 1988-89
NBA titles None
Ones to watch Alonzo Mourning, Larry Johnson, Tyrone "Muggsy" Bogues

CHICAGO BULLS
Franchise history Began as expansion team in 1966-67
NBA titles Won NBA Championships in 1991, 1992 and 1993
Ones to watch Michael Jordan, Scottie Pippen, Toni Kukoc

CLEVELAND CAVALIERS
Franchise history Began as expansion franchise in 1970-71
NBA titles None
Ones to watch Terrell Brandon, Tyrone Hill, Dan Majerle

DALLAS MAVERICKS
Franchise history Began as expansion team in 1980-81
NBA titles None
Ones to watch Jason Kidd, Jamal Mashburn, Jim Jackson

DENVER NUGGETS
Franchise history Joined league from ABA in 1976-77
NBA titles None
Ones to watch Dikembe Mutombo, Antonio McDyess, Mahmoud Abdul-Rauf

DETROIT PISTONS
Franchise history Joined NBA in 1948-49 as Fort Wayne Pistons, became Detroit Pistons in 1957-58
NBA titles Won NBA Championships in 1989 and 1990
Ones to watch Grant Hill, Joe Dumars, Otis Thorpe

GOLDEN STATE WARRIORS
Franchise history Charter member as Philadelphia Warriors in 1946-47, became San Francisco Warriors in 1962-63 and Golden State Warriors in 1971-72
NBA titles Won NBA Championships in Philadelphia in 1947 and 1956; won NBA Championship in Golden State in 1975
Ones to watch Joe Smith, Tim Hardaway, Latrell Sprewell

HOUSTON ROCKETS
Franchise history Began as expansion San Diego Rockets in 1967-68; moved to Houston for 1971-72
NBA titles Won NBA Championships in 1994 and 1995
Ones to watch Hakeem Olajuwon, Clyde Drexler, Robert Horry

INDIANA PACERS
Franchise history Joined league from ABA in 1976-77
NBA titles None
Ones to watch Reggie Miller, Rik Smits, Derrick McKey

LOS ANGELES CLIPPERS
Franchise history Buffalo Braves began as expansion franchise in 1970-71, became San Diego Clippers in 1978-79, moved to Los Angeles for 1984-85
NBA titles None
Ones to watch Lamond Murray, Pooh Richardson, Loy Vaught

LOS ANGELES LAKERS
Franchise history Joined NBA in 1948-49 as Minneapolis Lakers, became Los Angeles Lakers in 1960-61
NBA titles Won NBA Championships in Minneapolis in 1949, 1950, 1952, 1953 and 1954; won NBA Championships in Los Angeles in 1972, 1980, 1982, 1985, 1987 and 1988
Ones to watch Nick Van Exel, Cedric Ceballos, Vlade Divac

MIAMI HEAT
Franchise history Began as expansion team in 1988-89
NBA titles None
Ones to watch New coach Pat Riley, Glen Rice, Billy Owens

MILWAUKEE BUCKS
Franchise history Began as expansion team in 1968-69
NBA titles Won NBA Championship in 1971
Ones to watch Glenn Robinson, Shawn Respert, Vin Baker

MINNESOTA TIMBERWOLVES
Franchise history Began as expansion team in 1989-90
NBA titles None
Ones to watch Kevin Garnett, Isaiah Rider, Christian Laettner

NEW JERSEY NETS
Franchise history Joined league from ABA in 1976-77 as New York Nets, became New Jersey Nets in 1977-78
NBA titles None
Ones to watch Derrick Coleman, Kenny Anderson, Ed O'Bannon

NEW YORK KNICKS
Franchise history Charter member in 1946-47
NBA titles Won NBA Championships in 1970 and 1973
Ones to watch Patrick Ewing, John Starks, Charles Oakley

ORLANDO MAGIC
Franchise history Began as expansion team in 1989-90
NBA titles None
Ones to watch Shaquille O'Neal, Anfernee Hardaway, Horace Grant

PHOENIX SUNS
Franchise history Began as expansion franchise in 1968-69
NBA titles None
Ones to watch Charles Barkley, Kevin Johnson, Danny Manning

PORTLAND TRAIL BLAZERS
Franchise history Began as expansion franchise in 1970-71
NBA titles Won NBA Championship in 1977
Ones to watch Clifford Robinson, Rod Strickland, Randolph Childress

PHILADELPHIA 76ERS
Franchise history Joined NBA as Syracuse Nationals in 1949-50, became Philadelphia 76ers in 1963-64
NBA titles Won NBA Championship in Syracuse in 1955 and in Philadelphia in 1967 and 1983
Ones to watch Shawn Bradley, Jerry Stackhouse, Clarence Weatherspoon

SACRAMENTO KINGS
Franchise history Joined NBA in 1948-49 as Rochester Royals, became Cincinnati Royals in 1957-58, became Kansas City-Omaha Kings in 1972-73, became Kansas City Kings in 1975-76, became Sacramento Kings in 1985-86
NBA titles Won NBA Championship in Rochester in 1951
Ones to watch Mitch Richmond, Brian Grant, Walt Williams

SAN ANTONIO SPURS
Franchise history Joined league from ABA in 1976-77
NBA titles None
Ones to watch David Robinson, Sean Elliot, Avery Johnson

SEATTLE SUPERSONICS
Franchise history Joined NBA as expansion team in 1967-68
NBA titles Won NBA Championship in 1979
Ones to watch Shawn Kemp, Gary Payton, Detlef Schrempf

TORONTO RAPTORS
Franchise history Began as expansion team in 1995-96
NBA titles None
Ones to watch Damon Stoudamire, Alvin Robertson, Willie Anderson

UTAH JAZZ
Franchise history New Orleans Jazz joined league as expansion team in 1974-75, moved to Utah for 1979-80
NBA titles None
Ones to watch Karl Malone, John Stockton, Jeff Hornacek

VANCOUVER GRIZZLIES
Franchise history Began as expansion team in 1995-96
NBA titles None
Ones to watch Bryant Reeves, Lawrence Moten, Greg Anthony

WASHINGTON BULLETS
Franchise history Began as expansion team Chicago Packers in 1961-62 season, became Chicago Zephyrs in 1962-63, became Baltimore Bullets in 1963-64 season, became Capital Bullets in 1973-74 season and Washington Bullets in 1974-75
NBA titles Won NBA Championship in 1978
Ones to watch Chris Webber, Juwan Howard, Calbert Cheaney

Everyone who comes away from an NBA game will recall a moment when he or she connected with the action. Closeups on the giant, ultra-clear television screens make the arenas seem like living rooms. The seats that border the playing surface are unheard of in other venues. They afford a chance to look into the eyes of the players, to see the strain of competition and the enthusiasm they have for the game.

Possessing the grace of gazelles in full flight, there can be little argument that the men who populate NBA rosters are indeed among the greatest athletes in the world. They play at a breakneck speed. Much of the game is played off the floor in mid-air, twisting and turning and pausing and shooting and rebounding in defiance of the laws of gravity. They bang big, muscled bodies under the basket. The game is as physical as it is fast.

As a total package, the NBA offers an unparalleled combination of superlative athletes and intense drama that makes it the most exciting game of our time.

"We happen to have a sport that happens to have the best athletes in the world, and you see them more intimately than in many other sports," Stern says. No helmets, no long sleeves, no long pants, and the best seat in the house is one that's liable to find you with an athlete in your lap.

And the person sitting in your lap could very well be one of the game's stars who has dominated the league since its inception. From George Mikan through Wilt Chamberlain and Julius Erving to the greats of today, the league has always had marquee players who have been called upon to carry the banner for the league. There are few sports fans who don't know who David Robinson is, fewer still who wouldn't recognize Charles Barkley or Shaquille O'Neal or Scottie Pippen, and especially Michael Jordan. It is a star-driven league, and there have never been more stars.

The brightest star by far is still Jordan, the basketball-player-turned-baseball-player-turned-basketball-player whose tongue-flapping, gravity-defying skills have captured the imagination of every person who has ever seen him play. His flights of fancy from the free-throw line have enraptured an entire generation of young sports fans. His effortless drives down the lane defy description. Fans are left with mouths agape, commentators struggle to find suitable adjectives, and even opponents marvel at his brilliance.

left: *Heir ascendant: Since winning Rookie-of-the-Year honours in 1993, Shaquille O'Neal has soared to headliner status on the NBA marquee. His Magic prevailed over Jordan's Bulls in the 1995 playoffs.* right: *Shaq attaq: Shaq's backboard-rattling dunks propelled him to the NBA scoring title in 1994-95.*

Off the court, the multi-talented Shaq is also a rap musician and a budding actor. His mammoth stature and infectious grin have made him second only to Michael Jordan in endorsement contracts.

Jordan was one of the first to bring a truly amazing grace to the broadening NBA stage. At just six foot six, he can seemingly fly to the basket; his hang time is unprecedented. Sure, people in the past could jump, but few can take off from the free-throw line like Jordan, stay in the air for what seems to be an eternity and throw the ball down with grace and style. His efforts in the NBA's Slam Dunk competition during All-Star breaks were truly memorable and showcased his athletic grace in the perfect forum – centre stage, with no one else on the court.

During games, from his guard position he can sky over opponents who dare to sit back and challenge him to come to the basket. If someone comes out to play him up-close, he uses his spectacular first-step quickness to beat them to the basket.

His unique talents have set the parameters all other guards try to match these days. In order to equal Jordan – and no one else has succeeded – players have been forced to get quicker, jump higher and stretch their athletic limits. The prototypical shooting guard has been redesigned in Jordan's image.

Tipping the other end of the scale is O'Neal, all seven feet and 301 pounds of him. He blasts past opponents to the net and dunks with a ferocity few thought possible. He plays the big man's game, hard, tough, in-your-face, take-no-prisoners. One of the most marvellous physical specimens ever to play the game, he stands on the verge of a career that could dwarf the efforts of all other big men.

O'Neal, who averaged 29.3 points and 11.4 rebounds per game in the 1994-95 season, has taken his game to new heights in just three seasons in the NBA. Where he was once just a dunker and an intimidating physical presence, he has since added short jump hooks and fall-away baseline jumpers to his arsenal, making him all the more dangerous. If he ever becomes even an average foul shooter, his scoring totals could soar.

In a bygone era Bill Russell had his Wilt Chamberlain. Today, O'Neal has a trio of centres who provide a constant challenge and give the Orlando Magic pivot a standard against which his developing game can be measured.

facing page: *Summit meeting: Shaq and Hakeem Olajuwon tip off at centre court at Houston's Summit arena during last year's finals.* top: *The Dream: Hakeem Olajuwon is considered by many to be the best in the game today.* bottom left: *Olajuwon drives around David Robinson of the San Antonio Spurs.* bottom right: *Underdogs from the start of the 1995 playoffs, the Rockets upset teams with the best four records in the regular season (Utah, Phoenix, San Antonio and Orlando) on their way to defending their NBA Championship.*

At the top of this group is the Nigerian-born Hakeem Olajuwon, who has carried the Houston Rockets to two consecutive NBA titles. "The Dream," as he's known, has starred in the NBA for more than a decade after gaining national recognition on the University of Houston's "Phi Slamma Jamma" teams. He's become the most complete centre in the game. At seven feet, 255 pounds, he runs the floor like a guard, has the silky smooth turnaround jump shot of a forward, and was the league's Most Valuable Player and Defensive Player of the Year in 1994, as well as the MVP of the NBA Finals back-to-back in 1994 and 1995.

Rounding out the quartet of established, dominant centres are David "The Admiral" Robinson of the San Antonio Spurs, and Patrick Ewing of the New York Knicks – teammates on the 1992 Dream Team, and fierce competitors on the NBA court.

Robinson, a six-year NBA veteran, got off to a delayed start on his career, spending two years in the U.S. Navy after graduating from the Naval Academy in 1987. It hasn't slowed him down much, as he has been on the Western Conference All-Star team each of his six seasons. He is a mobile centre, able to bang inside or play outside, giving defenders fits.

While Olajuwon has two NBA titles, and O'Neal and the Magic appear to be on the verge of a possible dynasty, Robinson has piled up some impressive individual credentials in San Antonio. He was the league's leading scorer in the 1993-94 season, averaging 29.8 points per game and solidifying his hold on the title with a brilliant 71-point effort against the Los Angeles Clippers on the final day of that regular season. In 1994-95, Robinson was the regular season MVP, averaging 27.6 points per game and appearing in 81 of the 82 regular season contests. The only thing he hasn't done is win an NBA title, but the Spurs enter each season as one of the favourites for the Western Conference crown.

Patrick Ewing has been the acknowledged leader of the New York Knicks and a force in the NBA since the day he left Georgetown University. Ewing lacks only an NBA Championship to put the icing on an illustrious career. A classic back-to-the-basket centre, he battles inside with ferocity on defence and is the go-to man on the New York offence. His turnaround jump shot has become among the best in the game.

far left: *Very emotional and animated on the court, Alonzo Mourning is the Charlotte Hornets' leading rebounder and a fierce competitor.*
left: *Strength against strength: When Shaq and Nugget's Dikembe Mutombo meet under the basket, it's a classic confrontation of the league's best offensive player against one of its best on defence.*
facing page: *A standout since winning Rookie-of-the-Year honours in 1990, David Robinson is the heart and soul of the San Antonio Spurs. In 1994-95 he led his team to the best regular season record – 62 wins and 20 losses.*

top (left to right): *Assistant coaches Mike Krzyzewski and Lenny Wilkens; Michael Jordan, Larry Bird, Magic Johnson, Chris Mullin, Clyde Drexler, John Stockton, P. J. Carlesimo.* bottom: *Scottie Pippen, Christian Laettner, Patrick Ewing, Head Coach Chuck Daly, David Robinson, Karl Malone, Charles Barkley.*

THE DREAM TEAM

The decision to allow NBA professionals to compete in the 1992 Summer Olympic Games provided the NBA and the sport with a global opportunity to spread the gospel of basketball, and the worldwide congregation soaked it up.

Magic, Michael and Larry; Sir Charles, The Admiral and The Mailman; Ewing, Pippen, Drexler, Stockton, Mullin and Laettner. They were members of that Dream Team, and they did more for the game through the 1992 Barcelona Olympics than any team had done for a sport at any time in the past.

"Some day, they're liable to talk about Before Dream Team and After Dream Team," NBA Commissioner David Stern says when talking about the impact the collection of stars will have on the worldwide acceptance of the sport. "It was the defining moment on the global basketball scene. It made Olympic basketball one of the pillars of Olympic competition, and it wasn't that way before the Dream Team."

The scene whenever the Dream Team played was incredible. Star-struck fans cheered from the far-flung reaches of Portland's Memorial Coliseum, where the team played the qualification event, to the top rows of the arena in Barcelona, Spain, the site of the Olympic tournament itself. The players spent the pre-Olympic period ensconced in Monte Carlo, a perfect location befitting basketball royalty. Public appearances were as one would expect – a mob scene of kids and adults trying to get close to heroes they had never before seen in person. A stroll by Charles Barkley down the jam-packed Las Ramblas tourist track in Barcelona was nothing more than a Royal Walkabout conducted by one of the Kings of the Court. At the opening ceremonies in Barcelona, Magic Johnson was mobbed by fellow athletes.

In addition to taking the game to unprecedented heights in popularity, the all-star collection of players took the game to new levels on the floor.

The Dream Team was the perfect basketball machine, the gifted Johnson at point guard directing an awesome offence with his array of no-look passes and fast-break baskets. He could dish off to the high-flying Jordan, hit Bird or Mullin in the corner for a three-pointer or catch Pippen or Malone or Drexler trailing the break. The team could pound it inside to Ewing or Robinson, neither of whom was ever guarded by a player of similar skills. The Dream Team won its games at the Olympics by an average margin of 43.8 points and scored 117.9 points per game. The closest anyone came was in the gold medal game when Croatia – with NBA regulars Dino Radja and Toni Kukoc – stayed within 32 points, a moral victory of sorts.

SALARY CAPS AND THE DRAFT LOTTERY

They are two uniquely NBA processes that allow the league to stand out from all other professional sports organizations. They exist to promote some sense of parity among the member clubs, and how they are managed goes a long way in determining a franchise's fate. They are the salary cap and the draft lottery, and they're as important as shooting and ball-handling in the grand scheme of things.

The cap sets a specific dollar total – which changes year to year depending on team and league revenues – that can be spent on player salaries. It will crack the $20-million barrier in the 1995-96 season. Every team must manage the cap to keep the players it wants and go after the ones it desires. There are ways to manoeuvre within the cap that make this task even more important. It is a complicated procedure that teams are always thinking about when they are restructuring the contracts of players they already have or are negotiating with free agents they want.

The Raptors and Grizzlies are limited by their expansion agreements to spending just two-thirds of the league cap in their first year, three-quarters in their second and then the full amount in their third season.

While the salary cap is an exercise in advanced bookkeeping, the draft lottery is easier to understand, and plays a key role in the have-nots of the league hoping to become the haves. And, in typical NBA fashion, it has become an event. Each of the teams that misses the playoffs has a chance to win the lottery and choose the first overall pick in that year's draft. The nationally televised lottery is weighted so that the team with the worst record has the best chance of winning. However, if either Toronto or Vancouver wins the lottery before 1999, they will be moved to second in the draft and the second place team gets the first pick. If they finish one-two, the third place lottery team is the lucky winner.

The lottery was invented in 1985 to ensure that once teams had been eliminated from the playoff race, their drafting position would not be solely affected by their final record. Patrick Ewing of Georgetown University was the first lottery pick in history, and has gone on to greatness with the Knicks. The best lottery luck so far has belonged to the Orlando Magic, who won in both 1992 and 1993. With the first year's pick, they chose Shaquille O'Neal of Louisiana State University, and took Chris Webber of Michigan (above) the next season, dealing the latter to Golden State for Penny Hardaway. With O'Neal and Hardaway, Orlando vaulted ahead of many established teams to become a serious contender for the NBA title.

As centres become the focal point of many teams, there are other contenders trying to join O'Neal, Olajuwon, Robinson and Ewing in the superstar category. Two in particular are not that far away.

Alonzo Mourning of the Charlotte Hornets, the smallest of this group at six foot 10, has made big strides in the NBA after leaving Georgetown University only three seasons ago. Mourning, who is an NBA national spokesman against child abuse, is developing an intense rivalry with O'Neal, buoyed by the fact they play in the same conference and see each other four times a season. "'Zo," who has twice led the Hornets to post-season appearances, paced the team in scoring and rebounding in the 1994-95 season, and seems destined for future greatness.

Another of those Georgetown greats is Denver's Dikembe Mutombo, a native of Zaire who is one of the game's pre-eminent defenders. A brilliant shot-blocker whose defensive skills are similar to those of Russell in his era with the Celtics, Dikembe Mutombo Mpolondo Mukamba Jean Jacque Wamutombo is becoming one of the most feared centres in the league.

In 1994-95, he led the league in shotblocking, and was second in rebounds per game – trailing only Dennis Rodman and placing ahead of Shaquille O'Neal.

facing page: For the past decade, the New York Knicks' offence has revolved around Patrick Ewing's strong low post play.

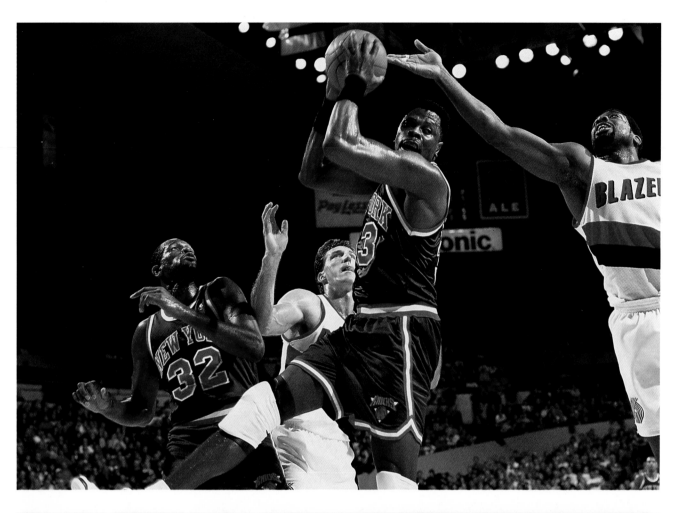

left: *A perennial league leader in shotblocking, Denver Nuggets' Mutombo is considered one of the top defenders in the league.* right: *Alonzo Mourning throws downs a ferocious reverse jam.* facing page: *At six foot nine, Larry Johnson may tower over five-foot-three Tyrone "Muggsy" Bogues, but make no mistake, Bogues is the floor leader for the Charlotte Hornets.*

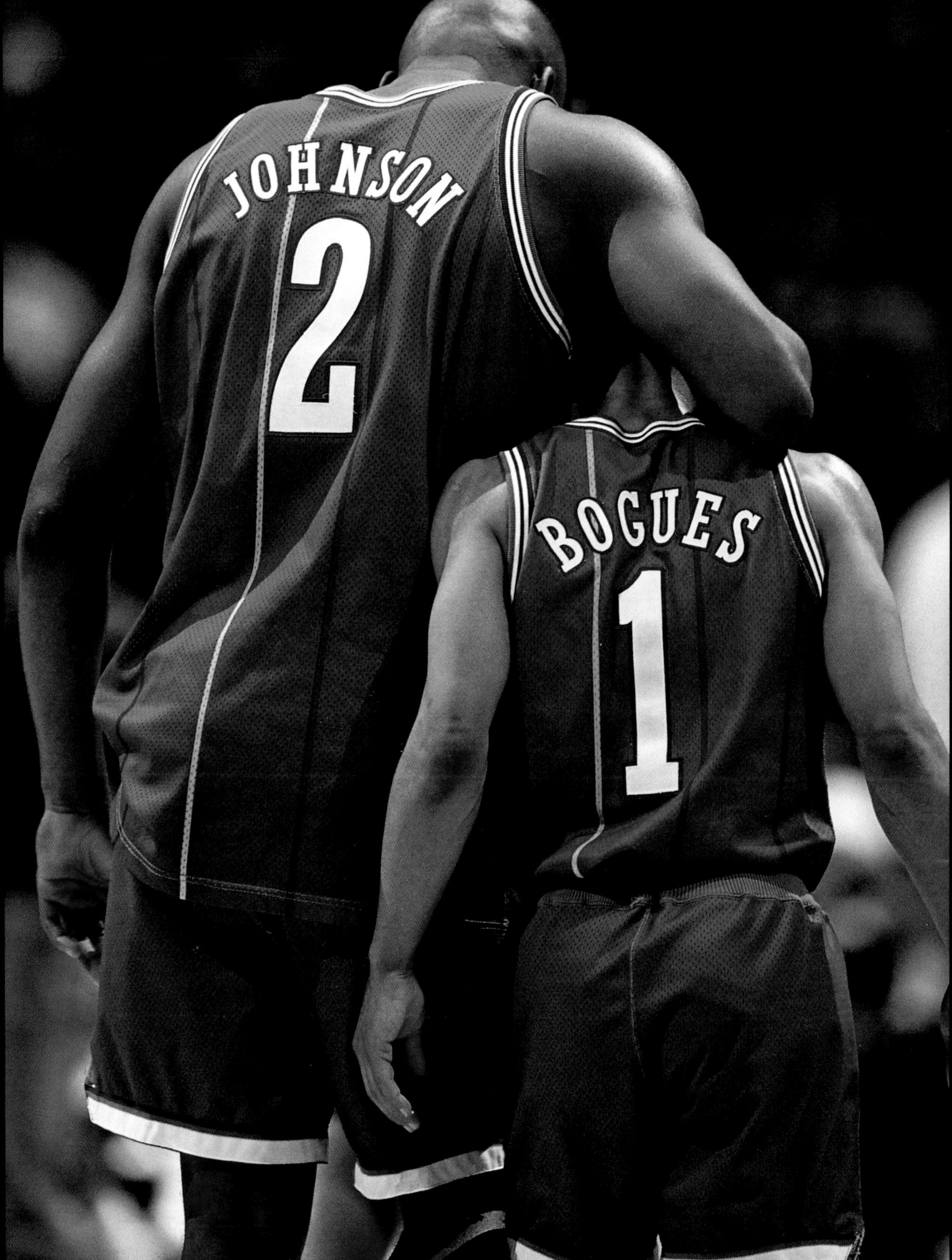
JOHNSON
2
BOGUES
1

ELITE FEET

They are the backbones of multi-million dollar businesses, they are fashion statements and important parts of worldwide marketing efforts.

They are basketball shoes and they are much, much more than footwear.

In the days of yore, the shoes worn by basketball stars were simple, black canvas, cut high above the ankles and adorned with nothing but eyelets for the laces.

Today, they are space-age high-tech pieces of equipment, delicately balanced for weight, support and arch support. They are also, of course, designed to catch the eyes and pocketbooks of teenagers and their parents all across the world. Shoe contracts can surpass playing contracts for some of today's NBA players and most advertising campaigns include a player-spokesman. Shoes have become an integral part of the game and the business these days. And they've provided a few interesting moments of late:

Great Moments in Footwear I: Michael Jordan is fined $5,000 for wearing white sneakers with black trim rather than black sneakers with white trim as the rest of his Chicago Bulls teammates do during the 1994-95 season.

Great Moments in Footwear II: Dennis Rodman incurs the wrath of San Antonio Spurs coach Bob Hill and a couple of teammates for taking off his shoes and lying on the floor, after being lifted from a playoff game last year.

Great Moments in Footwear III: Scottie Pippen, in one of the most memorable moments of sartorial splendour, is named the Most Valuable Player of the 1994 All-Star Game after scoring 29 points bedecked in a pair of the most garish red shoes known to man. "I definitely think it was the shoes. I think everybody was looking at my feet and I was able to shoot the ball well," he joked.

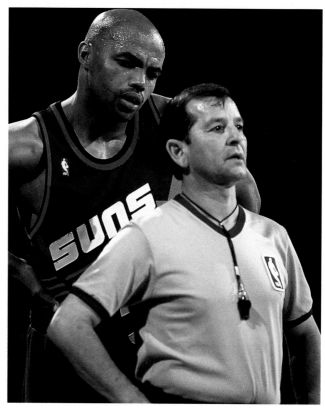

All hail the Sun King! On offence, defence or in the media,
Phoenix Suns' Charles Barkley is never afraid to let his emotion
show. You never have to guess what Sir Charles is feeling.

Two of the most gifted and colourful players of all time are plying their trade in today's NBA, and people watch them as much for what they might say as for what they might do. Charles Barkley of the Phoenix Suns and Dennis Rodman of the Chicago Bulls are a couple of basketball-playing iconoclasts who are as unpredictable off the court as they are on it.

Barkley has electrified the NBA since leaving from Auburn University in 1984. Well-spoken, but ever outspoken, the six-foot-five forward remains a highly quotable figure who is never shy about speaking his mind. Although many of his off-court actions and comments have given him a rebellious image, Barkley also works silently behind the scenes helping the less fortunate, visiting hospitals and doing countless hours of anonymous charity work. He is an enigma whose public persona does not reveal the man within.

On the court, Barkley is one of the game's greats. Despite his relative lack of height, he is one of the best rebounders in the game and a scoring machine who mixes it up with bigger foes every night. He has made the Suns a legitimate NBA title contender since being traded from Philadelphia, helping Phoenix reach the Finals against Chicago in 1993.

His drive to win manifests itself in many ways. He's not afraid to take both referees and teammates to task for mistakes in crucial games.

Barkley came out of college as the "Round Mound of Rebound," with tons of potential and what looked like an appetite to match. He worked on his game with his typical ferocity and culminated his development by being named the league's Most Valuable Player in 1993, his first season with the Suns. Barkley has said that he harbours hopes of a political career after his playing days are done, perhaps as governor of his home state of Alabama. Barkley in a government leadership role would be an interesting spectacle.

If colourful is the figurative adjective we use to describe Barkley, it's a literal description of Rodman, the man of many hair hues. While no one questions his abilities – a two-time NBA champion with the Detroit Pistons, one of the best rebounders the game has ever seen, with four straight NBA rebounding titles to prove it – he is as famous for his behaviour off the court, and that sometimes takes away from true appreciation for the gifts he has as a player. At just six foot eight, "The Worm," as he is known, battles bigger, stronger men for rebounds and nearly always wins. Unselfish almost to a fault at the offensive end of the court, Rodman often waits patiently on the wing for his teammates to run plays. But, once the ball hits the backboard or basket, he pounces like a lion on raw meat. He thinks every loose ball is his, and often it is.

Rodman is likely to show up with red hair one day, gold hair the next, green the day after that in his march to his own personal drummer. His pierced body, many and varied tattoos and personality have given him a special place in the NBA world. He has dated pop singer Madonna, was a presenter at the 1995 MTV awards, and reaches a hip, younger, non-traditional basketball audience. As Toronto Raptors Coach Brendan Malone, who was an assistant with the Pistons during Rodman's tenure, once said: "I'd like to get inside his head and see how he sees the world. But not for long, mind you."

That Rodman played on the same team with the conservative David Robinson was one of the great and intriguing mixes of personalities in all of sports. However, their diverse work ethics and comportment cost "The Worm" his employment in San Antonio just before the season began when he was dealt to the Chicago Bulls in a giveaway for backup centre Will Perdue. Now he must fit in with Michael Jordan and the rest of the Bulls in Chicago. "It's a decision that's important to the franchise. We felt we had to weigh it out, think about it. I got to know a little about Dennis, that he's overcome a lot of odds. He's an awful strong individual and I'm confident he will take himself out of situations that have been tough for him his whole life," was how Chicago coach Phil Jackson summed up the deal.

Basketball is, and always will be, a team game in which five players working in symphony are necessary for victory. While a single star may capture the imagination of the fans, true success comes from teamwork – a great outside shooter with a dominant inside player, speed combined with strength, great starters with an excellent bench. Teams that have won in the past, and will win in the future, are finely tuned machines working absolutely in sync.

There are several sets of teammates in today's NBA who play off each other and complement each other's talents so well that the sum is far greater than the individual parts.

far left: *Free spirit: Dennis Rodman will tell fans what he's thinking after any play – good or bad.*
left: *The many hues of Dennis Rodman; this time it's blond.*
facing page: *A two-time NBA Defensive Player of the Year, Rodman grabs a rebound in his signature style.*

eft: *Still near the top of his game after 10 years in the league, Karl Malone is the game's*
premier power forward. top right: *Teammate John Stockton, the NBA's all-time assists*
leader, drives on the Magic. bottom right: *Jazz combo: In Stockton and Malone Utah*
boasts one of the best guard-forward combinations ever.

Karl Malone and John Stockton of the Utah Jazz are a perfect illustration of teammates working to near perfection. Ever since Malone was picked in the first round of the 1985 draft (a year after Stockton was taken in the first round of the 1984 draft), the duo has been working as one.

The powerful Malone, nicknamed "The Mailman" because he always delivers, is the all-time leading scorer in Jazz history, thanks mainly to Stockton, who is the career-assists leader in the NBA. A six-foot-nine forward, who also leads the Jazz in career rebounding, field goals made and attempted, and free throws made and attempted, Malone is one of the quiet superstars of the league, which has as much to do with the relatively small media market he plays in than anything else. He made a huge impact on the Dream Team at the Barcelona Olympics, and will play again on the team at the 1996 Atlanta Olympics.

But Malone without Stockton is nearly incomprehensible to NBA fans, so linked are the two. Stockton, like Malone a Dream Teamer in 1992, and in 1996 as well, passed Magic Johnson last season to take over the NBA career lead in assists. The six-foot-one graduate of tiny Gonzaga University is one of the most unselfish players in the game, always looking to make the great pass, a pass that often ends with a dunk or a layup for Malone.

THE COMMISSIONERS

From the time it was the Basketball Association of America with 11 teams anchored on the eastern seaboard, until a time when its players and teams are familiar and appreciated on every corner of the earth, only four men have held the NBA's mantle of command.

David Stern (above), Larry O'Brien, J. Walter Kennedy and Maurice Podoloff have been responsible for overseeing the transformation of the NBA from its origins in 1946 through to the present day. Generally considered the most savvy of all the commissioners of major sports leagues today, Stern began his tenure in 1984 after being the league's general counsel and vice president in charge of business and legal affairs. His time at the helm has been one of unprecedented popularity of the game.

Stern took over from Larry O'Brien, who served from 1975 to 1984. One of O'Brien's major tasks was helping speed along the merger between the NBA and the upstart American Basketball Association. O'Brien's ties to the political world – he was chairman of the Democratic party and an advisor to John F. Kennedy – helped immensely as the league was able to obtain approval from Congress for the 1976 union.

The biggest growth spurt in league history came under the eyes of J. Walter Kennedy, who was in charge from 1963 to 1975 and watched the league double in size from nine to 18 teams.

The task of getting the fractured basketball community to work for the common good in the infancy of the Basketball Association of America and the NBA fell to Maurice Podoloff, who guided the ship from 1946 to 1963. Podoloff was a Yale-educated lawyer born in Czarist Russia who had the necessary sports expertise when the league came calling. His connections were invaluable – he had been president of the American Hockey League, and his family owned New Haven Arena in Connecticut.

Podoloff convinced teams from the Midwest-based National Basketball League to join forces with the BAA in the late 1940s, a move that solidified the sport's base and set the stage for the development that continues today.

following pages: *Karl Malone goes in strong against the Lakers.*

While there have been no NBA Championships for the duo to celebrate, they did enjoy a memorable day on the national stage in 1993 when they were named co-winners of the Most Valuable Player award in the NBA's All-Star Game, a game that was played on their home court in Salt Lake City.

While Malone and Stockton have been creating their Utah magic for a decade, a new guard-forward tandem is rising in the Pacific Northwest. Shawn Kemp and Gary Payton of the Seattle SuperSonics represent the new wave of teammates who fill highlight reels night after night.

Kemp, who was one of the big fan favourites of the Dream Team at the World Championship of Basketball in Toronto in 1994, is one of the most acrobatic forwards in the game today. Despite not having played college basketball – he spent one year at junior college but did not play – he is one of the crowd favourites wherever he plays, primarily due to the intense emotions he shows after his thundering dunks leave opponents stunned and wondering what just hit them. He is power personified, six foot 10 and 245 pounds of muscle barrelling over anyone who gets in his way.

His power is augmented by the lightning quickness of his teammate Payton. After four years in the league, Payton, a six-foot-four guard, is developing into one of the game's pre-eminent defenders, able to strip opponents of the ball time and time again with hands and feet as fast as light. A two-time All-Star, he is the perfect complement to Kemp, and together they give the SuperSonics one of the most impressive young duos in the game.

Adding to the Sonics' emergence as one of the NBA's best teams is forward Detlef Schrempf. A former two-time winner of the Sixth Man of the Year award at Indiana, Schrempf has blossomed into an all-star starting forward whose game has improved every year since arriving in Seattle. One of the NBA's great playmaking forwards and an adept ball-handler, Schrempf is also a constant threat from beyond the three-point line. He finished second only to Steve Kerr of Chicago in three-point field goal accuracy during the past season and has proved himself to be the Sonics' most consistent player, night in and night out.

Seattle SuperSonics pose a triple threat to opponents.
facing page: *Sonics on-court leader Shawn Kemp posted top-10 numbers in field goal percentage and rebounding for the 1994-95 season. Here, he leaves the Mavericks flatfooted.*
far left: *Commanding presence of point guard Gary Payton leaves opponent's defence in tatters.*
left: *Three-point threat Detlef Schrempf turns the corner on the Knicks.*

A Kidd's game: Dallas fans have something to cheer about. In the last three years the Mavericks have acquired an all-star-calibre trio of young hot shots: Jason Kidd, Jim Jackson and Jamal Mashburn. Kidd possesses an inspired awareness of the floor and selfless passing skills which help the Mavericks make the most of their scoring opportunities.

Youth is also being served in Dallas, where the Mavericks are trying to escape from years of oblivion, powered by a tremendous trio of young talent in Jason Kidd, Jimmy Jackson and Jamal Mashburn. For years, the Mavericks were among the laughing stocks of the league, but their resurgence is being led by these three rising stars, who helped the team improve their win total by 23 games last season.

Jason Kidd, co-winner with Detroit's Grant Hill of the league's Rookie of the Year award in 1994-95 (the first co-winners since Dave Cowens and Geoff Petrie in the 1970-71 season), is another gifted passer in the Magic Johnson-John Stockton vein. Kidd led the league in triple doubles (points, assists and rebounds) and dazzled fans, players and coaches alike. Shooting guard, Jimmy Jackson is a complete player both offensively and defensively, and last season, before an ankle injury put him out of commission, he was the highest scoring non-centre in the league. Emerging as one of the league's premier power forwards in only his second year in the NBA, Jamal Mashburn finished fifth in scoring last season with a 24.1 points per game average.

Just as Kidd, Jackson and Mashburn are trying to lead the Mavericks to respectability, the team of Tim Hardaway, Latrell Sprewell and Chris Mullin are trying to accomplish the same feat with the Golden State Warriors, a team plagued by injuries and dissension in the last few years. Now that the Chris Webber-Don Nelson personality clash has been resolved with the trade of Webber to the Washington Bullets and Nelson's departure to coach the Knicks, Hardaway, Sprewell and Mullin will have to be the key ingredients to a Warriors resurgence. Hardaway possesses one of the game's singularly greatest moves with his cross-over dribble. The sheer speed of the move, moving a defender one way and then brilliantly cutting back to the other, is astonishing and will be Hardaway's legacy to the game. Sprewell, despite being a six-foot-five guard, can dunk with the best of them, and his explosions to the basket are memorable. The veteran Mullin, one of the game's best pure shooters, took his game to the world stage with the Dream Team in Barcelona, and, in combination with the quickness of Hardaway and Sprewell, keeps teams who want to focus on the other two honest.

A trio of rising stars has pulled the Mavericks into playoff contention. **left:** *All eyes are on Jason Kidd, consensus choice as a future superstar.* **top right:** *Power forward Jamal Mashburn shot a higher field-goal percentage than all-time greats Larry Bird and Charles Barkley did in their sophomore years.* **bottom right:** *Explosive guard Jimmy Jackson, teamed with Kidd, gives Dallas a potential Hall-of-Fame backcourt.*

left: *Latrell Sprewell twists for two. The volatile guard led Golden State scorers in 1994-95.* right: *MVP contender Scottie Pippen goes to the hoop with authority.*

right: *Determined veteran forward Chris Mullin hopes to lead the Warriors back to prominence.*
far right: *High-scoring point guard Tim Hardaway is the floor general for Golden State.*

The missing achievement in all of those sets of dominant teammates, however, is the ultimate goal – an NBA Championship. Neither Stockton and Malone, nor Kemp and Payton, nor Kidd, Jackson and Mashburn, nor Hardaway, Sprewell and Mullin have yet to get their teams to the top of the mountain.

One team player who has been to the summit and can't wait to get back there again is Scottie Pippen, the small forward/guard of the Chicago Bulls. A three-time NBA champion, a member of the 1992 Dream Team and next year's U.S. Olympic team, and arguably the best all-around player in the league, Pippen led the Bulls in points, rebounding, assists and minutes played last year and has one of the most complete games in the league. At six foot seven, he can post up guards, is comfortable playing the point or off-guard, and can move up to forward with ease. There are very few players in the game who can defend him, and on the defensive end of the floor, he's a demon, quicker than many forwards he matches up with, and bigger than the guards he opposes.

He also has a perfect foil in Croatian-born teammate Toni Kukoc, a six-foot-11 forward with great passing skills who is becoming more adept at the NBA style of game with every game played. Kukoc, who was on the Croatian team that lost the 1992 Olympic gold medal game to Pippen and the Dream Team, was a legendary star of the Italian professional league before jumping to the NBA. After some growing pains, he is becoming the player everyone thought he would be when he was wooed away from Europe.

But Pippen will always be remembered for the role he played in the Chicago Bulls dynasty of the early 1990s, a dynasty led by Michael Jordan, but one that wouldn't have existed without the contributions of Pippen and Horace Grant, the tireless power forward who is now making the Orlando Magic everyone's pick as the next dominant team.

The Pippen-Jordan championship teams of 1990-91, 1991-92 and 1992-93 represented a continuation of the multi-championship teams established in the 1980s by the Boston Celtics and Los Angeles Lakers, and continued by Isiah Thomas and the Detroit Pistons in the last two years of the decade.

From the Bulls, the torch has been passed to the Houston Rockets, the NBA champions of the last two seasons. The all-around brilliance of centre Hakeem Olajuwon has been the key, but last season's championship would not have been won without the contribution of Clyde "The Glide" Drexler, obtained in mid-season from the Portland Trail Blazers. Drexler, a teammate of Olajuwon's at the University of Houston, had a storied 11-year career with Portland but had never won a title. The sight of him standing on the floor amid the jubilation after the championship had been clinched was the crowning moment to a brilliant career.

But where will the next great team come from? With the wealth of burgeoning young talent spread throughout the league, that's an impossible question to answer, but there are a few solid bets out there.

The best chance is being given to the up-and-coming Orlando Magic, last season's losing finalists but a promising young team anchored by the imposing presence of Mr. O'Neal. But even the great Shaq can't accomplish the ultimate feat alone, and it is the supporting cast that gives rise to the optimism in central Florida.

facing page: *The Croatian sensation, versatile Toni Kukoc has found an NBA home in Chicago.* following pages, top: *Celtics and Magic square off in legendary Boston Garden.* following pages, bottom: *Home of the greatest dynasty in NBA history, the Garden saw its last game in spring 1995.*

THE CANADIANS

From three players who were in the league in its first year of existence to two playing the game today, the dozen Canadian-born men who have made it to the NBA run the gamut of skill and contribution. All have battled long odds to reach the pinnacle of their sport.

Rick Fox (left) and Bill Wennington (right) are two Canadians well versed in the ins and outs of life in the NBA, and played together for the Canadian National Team. Fox, a native of Toronto, was drafted by the Boston Celtics in 1991, and he was the first rookie to start opening night for the Celtics since Larry Bird in 1979. For Bill Wennington, the transition into the NBA was not so smooth. After six seasons as an under-valued player with Dallas and Sacramento, Wennington went to Italy to give his career a kick start. There he led his team to the Italian Championships. He returned to the NBA two years later and is now a strong and valued player with the Chicago Bulls.

For Mike Smrek, his seven years in the NBA left him with enduring memories – and two championship rings as the only Canadian-born player to ever win an NBA title, a feat he accomplished with the 1986-87 and 1987-88 Los Angeles Lakers, playing with Magic Johnson and Kareem Abdul-Jabbar, during the era known simply as Showtime.

Leo Rautins, who will serve as the TV colour analyst for Raptors games this winter, was another who made that quantum leap. A standout forward at Syracuse University, he was a first-round draft pick of the Philadelphia 76ers in 1983, at that time the first Canadian ever chosen in the first round of the draft.

Only five men have gone from the ranks of the Canadian university system to the NBA. Jim Zoet went from Lakehead University to the Detroit Pistons; Ron Crevier, from Montreal's Dawson College to Golden State and Detroit; while American-born Brian Heaney attended Acadia University and played with the Baltimore Bullets. Two of the three Canadians who played with the 1946-47 Toronto Huskies – Gino Sovran and Hank Biasatti – were graduates of Windsor's Assumption College.

The rest of the Canadians – Toronto's Rautins; Stewart Granger of Montreal; Lars Hansen of Port Coquitlam, B.C.; Bob Houbregs of Toronto and Vancouver's Norm Baker – all developed their skills at American schools, the breeding ground for NBA stars.

Dreams will always drive Canadians to U.S. colleges, where the level of play is consistently far better and where the NBA scouts turn their attention when assessing prospects. But these days, with the advent of the new Canadian franchises, there will be more Canadians dreaming those dreams than in the past.

Entertainment tonight! The NBA's celebrity status
draws Hollywood's glitterati.
far left: *Knicks super fan, film director Spike Lee,
trades taunts and cheers from his regular courtside
seat at Madison Square Garden.*
left: *Hollywood heavyweight Jack Nicholson
faithfully follows the Lakers at Forum home games.*

Gifted point guard Penny Hardaway, obtained from the Golden State Warriors for Chris Webber on a draft-night deal in 1993, is developing into the best at his position in the league. Hardaway combines a great shooting touch, great ball-handling skills and a maturity that belies his years. His skills complement O'Neal's physical domination of the game under the backboards, and with leadership provided by veteran forward Horace Grant the Magic are poised to take the final step.

There are a handful of other great, players looking for the right combination of teammates and chemistry that will allow them to challenge the league's elite squads. Among them is Reggie Miller of the Indiana Pacers, who took his team as far as the Conference Finals in 1995, finally getting past the substantial hurdle imposed by Patrick Ewing and the New York Knicks. Miller, a member of the 1994 Dream Team, is one of the most gifted three-point shooters to ever play the game and has a knack of hitting the big shot at the most crucial point of the game. In last year's playoffs, he scored eight points in the dying seconds of a game to beat the Knicks in one of the most impressive clutch performances ever witnessed. And the fact that it happened in Madison Square Garden in

front of diehard Knicks fans and movie director Spike Lee, the biggest Knicks fan of all, made it all the more exciting.

Waiting patiently in the wings is a group of exciting young players who hope to leave their mark on the league as the superstars of the 1990s.

"Big Dog," Milwaukee's Glenn Robinson, made a significant impact with the Bucks in his rookie campaign, and has the Milwaukee faithful thinking playoffs again. After a tremendous college career at Purdue, culminating with consensus NCAA Player-of-the-Year honours in 1994, Robinson led all NBA rookies in scoring.

But while the "Big Dog" is barking, he's not the only young Buck making some noise. Vin Baker, a rookie whose skills were questioned by some when he was chosen eighth overall in the 1993 draft from the lightly regarded University of Hartford program, has become a perfect partner for Robinson in an excellent Milwaukee front line. The six-foot-10 power forward started all 82 games for Milwaukee in 1994-95, averaging 17.7 points and 10.3 rebounds as he made his first appearance in an All-Star Game, and became one of the most pleasant surprises in the NBA.

top: *Savvy veteran Clyde "The Glide" Drexler, here driving around the Magic's Nick Anderson,*
helped Houston Rockets repeat as NBA champions in 1995. bottom: *Unstoppable point guard*
Penny Hardaway came to the Magic on a draft-day trade and has Orlando talking dynasty.

left: *Solid defender Horace Grant brings championship experience to the youthful Orlando Magic from his three NBA titles with Chicago.* right: *Explosive Indiana shooting guard Reggie Miller is a threat from inside or long distance. His Pacers are considered to be NBA champions in waiting.*

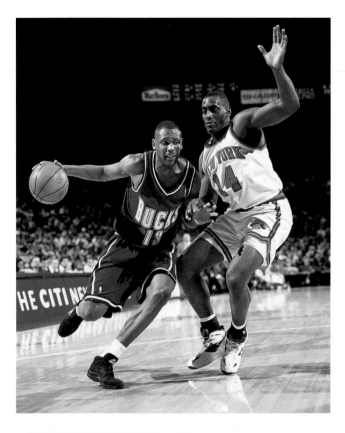

top left: *Highly touted rookie Glen "Big Dog" Robinson brings a complete game to the surging Milwaukee Bucks.* bottom left: *Robinson sets up for a two-handed power slam.* right: *All-star forward Vin Baker helps make the Milwaukee front line one of the best in the game.*

facing page: *Rookie sensation Grant Hill took the league by storm and is a fan favourite wherever he plays.*
left: *The future is bright for Grant Hill (left) and Jason Kidd, co-winners of the 1994-95 NBA Rookie-of-the-Year award.*

In Detroit, Grant Hill is a coach's delight as well as being one of the most engaging young players in the league. Just one year removed from a great career at Duke University, the son of former NFL running back Calvin Hill is ready to blossom. In his rookie season with the Pistons, Hill showed flashes of brilliance and a total game that includes taking the ball to the basket, the ability to pop out and hit jump shots, and a mature understanding of the nuances of the game. Coupled with a well-spoken nature, a clean-cut lifestyle and a sense of responsibility sadly lacking in some other young players, Hill has become a league favourite. Not only did he make the Eastern Conference All-Star starting line-up, he was the league leading vote-getter in fan balloting. No other rookie has ever achieved that milestone. The Pistons have high hopes for Hill as their leader for the future and a return to championship glory. His image is one of class, both on and off the court, making him the rare kind of athlete that seems to come along only once in a generation.

In Los Angeles, a resurgence of the Lakers is being led by one of the best young guards in the game, Nick Van Exel. At six foot one, the former Cincinnati star flourished under new coach Del Harris last year, and led the Lakers back to the playoffs, revitalizing the franchise along the way. A second-round pick of the 1993 draft who doesn't lack any confidence, he blossomed into an excellent scorer, averaging 16.9 points and 8.3 assists per game in 1994-95. Van Exel has a great supporting cast that includes rookie stand-out Eddie Jones, centre Vlade Divac and forward Cedric Ceballos.

Before being traded to Los Angeles, Ceballos never had the opportunity to truly showcase his talents. Playing a supporting role in Phoenix, it was difficult to crack the impressive cast of forwards in the Suns' line-up. The talent was there, but the numbers weren't in his favour. He has become an All-Star since being traded to the Lakers, and Jones, a former Temple star, was a strong contender for Rookie-of-the-Year honours in the 1994-95 season. Divac had his finest season as a pro in the 1994-95 season with career highs in scoring, blocks and assists. His assist total was the highest of all NBA centres and he was the only player in the league to have three 20-point, 20-rebound games last season.

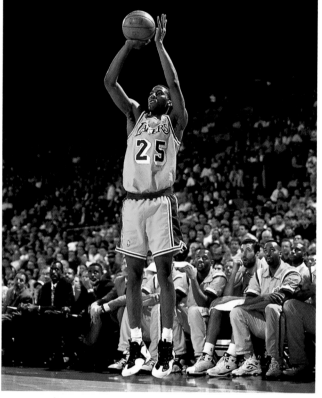

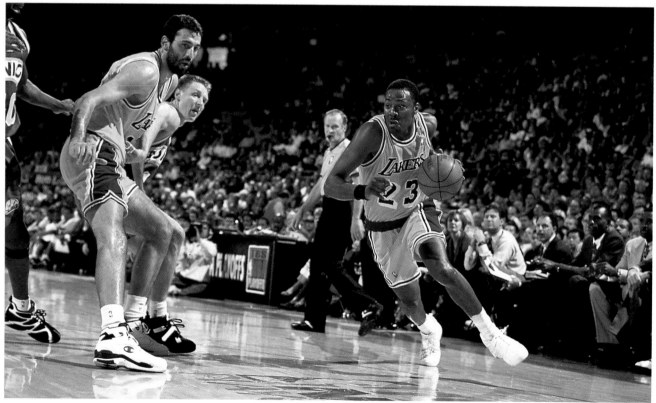

top left: *Laker guard Nick "The Quick" Van Exel blows past Dennis Rodman.*
top right: *Lakers 10th pick overall in the 1994 NBA draft, Eddie Jones blossomed into the Rookie All-Star Game MVP.* bottom: *Working off a pick by Vlade Divac, Cedric Ceballos drives to the basket.*

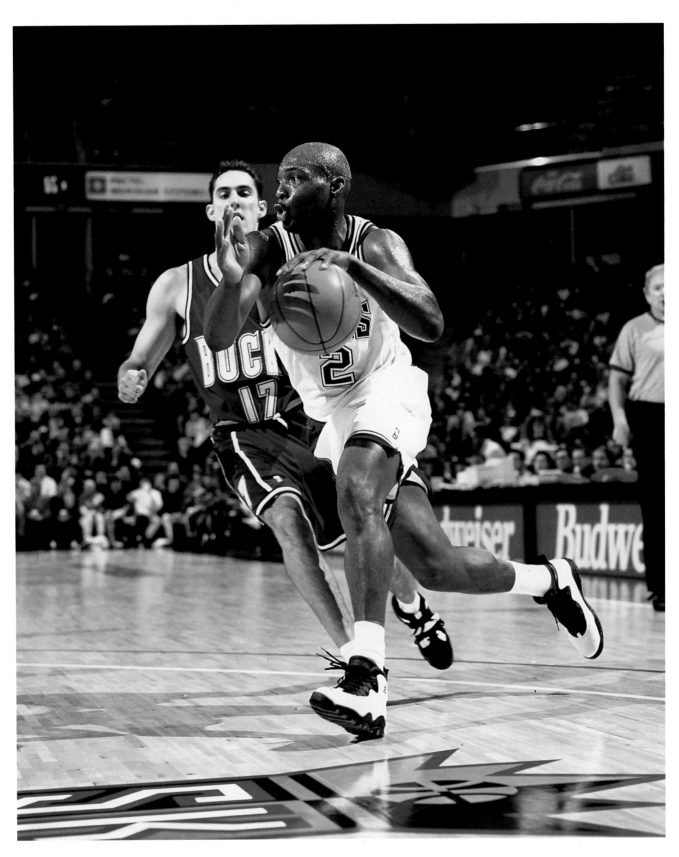

Sacramento scoring sensation Mitch Richmond en route to another two against Milwaukee.

In Sacramento, the long-suffering Kings fans are finally being rewarded with a much improved team. Led by shooting guard Mitch Richmond, the Kings now come to the court believing they can beat any team in the league. Richmond has represented the Kings in the All-Star Game for three straight years, winning the MVP award in last season's contest.

With the surprising emergence of rookies Brian Grant and Michael Smith, and solid play from third year man Walt Williams, youthful Sacramento is poised to return to the playoffs for the first time since 1986.

The contemporary NBA is flourishing: there are big men and small, deadly shooters and lightning-quick slashers, brilliant defenders and dominant rebounders. There are teams on the rise, players destined for greatness and rivalries developing that will be fought well into the next millennium.

The stunning growth over the last decade will be hard to match, but as the game branches out with expansion and an even greater world audience, the future looks bright indeed.

Some might argue that there has always been a Canadian flavour to the NBA. After all, James Naismith, the father of basketball, was born and raised in Canada. Maurice Podoloff, the league's first president, whose name graces the trophy awarded annually to the NBA's Most Valuable Player, was also a Canadian. Yet, until now, one key element was missing from the equation – Canadian fans have not had a team to call their own. But starting this season, the greats of the game will travel north to strut their finest across the hardwood.

The harsh glare of the spotlight will fall on the floor of Toronto's SkyDome this season as basketball fans wait to see which of the expansion Raptors becomes one of the stars of the next generation. The moment is full of promise, hope and excitement, and Raptors fans and team officials have every reason to feel confident.

The team, for its part, has embraced the community, igniting a spark of infectious enthusiasm and a quest for excellence. No one expects miracles, but the future is now for the Raptors, a future – like that of the NBA itself – full of promise and excitement.

OPENING NIGHT PASS

SEC	ROW	SEAT	PRICE
VIP	1	1	150.00

TORONTO RAPTORS
vs. NEW JERSEY NETS
FRI. NOV. 3, 1995 9:00 pm
SKYDOME
GATE

SEASON 01 | GAME 01

T H E

a b o v e : *The real credentials: Much-sought-after, the one-time-only souvenir laminated ticket was the passport to glory for fans attending Raptors' first regular season game, at Toronto's SkyDome, November 3, 1995, versus the New Jersey Nets.*

More than 21,000 people came to SkyDome, Wednesday, June 28, 1995, and saw a measure of legitimacy

RAPTORS

bestowed upon their newest sports team. After more than a year of hype surrounding the development and the naming of the franchise, the fans were finally to get a chance to see at least one of their players live and in person.

The evening was to be a defining moment in the construction of the basketball team, a night to pluck one of the most promising young athletes from the American college ranks and place upon him the mantle of leadership with a team starting from scratch.

There was an overwhelming sense of anticipation in the air as the curious fans filed into the downtown playpen on a sultry summer evening. The first NBA draft ever held outside of the United States and only the fourth to be held outside of the league's home in New York City was a glitzy and colourful affair. SkyDome was bedecked as never before. The Raptors' court, adorned with dinosaur paw prints, was laid down for all to see, and a stage that would do any Broadway production proud was set in the centre of the field. The franchise's dance team made a flashy debut, and the mascot was prancing and dancing and flying through the air in his first public appearance. Police tactical teams rappelled from the stadium roof, and music blared. It was a time for hoopla, and folks couldn't wait to find out which player would be theirs.

In the attached hotel a couple of storeys above the floor, in a meeting room connected to the outside world only by telephone lines and fax machines, Isiah Thomas had assembled his cabinet for the most important meeting he had ever chaired. For more than a year, Thomas and his trusted confidantes had criss-crossed North America evaluating talent, checking backgrounds and trying to predict the futures of would-be Raptors. The group had been studying for this day like it had studied for nothing before, and the importance of the moment was not lost on them. The names of the eligible players were written on boards that hung from the walls all around the scouts, player-personnel directors, video directors and coaches. Each had been carefully scrutinized; the men at those tables were intimately familiar with every single one of them.

On the floor, the evening was proceeding according to script. The best of the college players were being snapped up with predictable haste and in the order many expected. Joe Smith of Maryland would go first, Antonio McDyess of Alabama second and Jerry Stackhouse of North Carolina third. Another Tar Heel, Rasheed Wallace, would be the fourth selection of the draft and Kevin Garnett, an intriguing high school star, was snatched fifth.

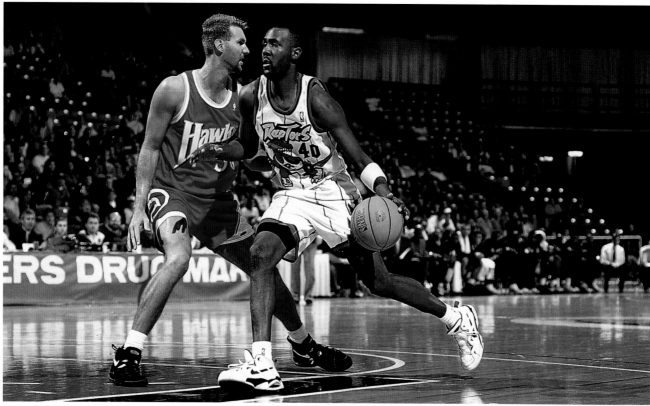

top: *A live stick of dynamite, energetic young Damon Stoudamire sets to explode to the hoop off his dribble.* bottom: *The Raptors will look to veteran Willie Anderson, a former standout with the Spurs, as their swingman. Here he drives on the Hawks.*

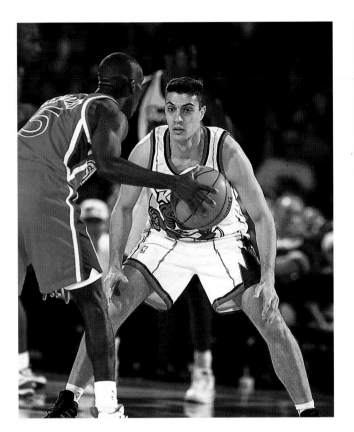

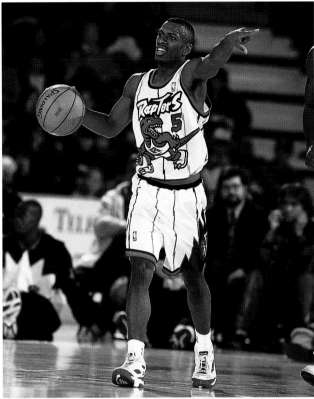

top left: *Learning to play defence the NBA way, Vincenzo Esposito bears down.* top right: *Chris Whitney directs traffic to set up the Raptors offence.* bottom left: *Jimmy King, the Raptors second-round pick in the college draft, puts the brakes on his dribble to evade a defender.* bottom right: *Tony Massenburg, here going up for a jumper versus the 76ers, impressed during pre-season play with his offensive attitude.*

left: *Power forward Tony Massenburg eludes the defence for a layup versus the Philadelphia 76ers in pre-season action.* right: *Former Houston Rockets centre Zan Tabak shows off his personal version of the Sky Hook.*

far left: *Toronto's first expansion draft pick B. J. Armstrong was a can't-lose proposition. If Armstrong stayed, he'd be a fine on-court leader. If he balked at reporting, the Raptors could demand plenty in a trade.*
left: *Isiah Thomas dealt Armstrong to Golden State for five players. The Raptors acquired Victor Alexander and Carlos Rogers, plus three second-round draft picks: Dwayne Whitfield, Martin Lewis and Michael McDonald. (From left: Alexander, Whitfield, Thomas, Lewis, Rogers.)*

That left just the Vancouver Grizzlies to pick before Thomas would get to make the biggest selection of his vice-presidential career, and the Grizzlies did what everyone expected, taking Bryant "Big Country" Reeves. Now it was Thomas' turn. History was about to be made.

Thomas knew exactly what he was doing when he made the call to the stage with the name of the anointed. He knew who he wanted, he knew why he wanted him, and he was genuinely pleased with the selection that was about to be made. Much had gone into the pick, much more than just the assessment of ball-handling, shooting, running and jumping skills. Thomas had a clearly defined path he wanted his team to take and he firmly believed this was the man to lead the way.

And still, there were as many boos as cheers when Commissioner David Stern announced to the hometown crowd that the Raptors had passed on crowd favourite Ed O'Bannon and chosen Arizona guard Damon Stoudamire as the first college draft pick in the franchise's history. But Isiah Thomas was not deterred.

The five-foot-10 guard shares many of the attributes Thomas had when he came out of Indiana in 1981. Stoudamire is a slasher, a penetrator who can make passes in traffic and possesses the skill to nail the three-pointer with alarming regularity. He was the co-Player of the Year in the PAC-10 along with UCLA's O'Bannon.

Stoudamire was a gutsy pick, the kind of bold move that can either work brilliantly or flame out in a storm of unrealized potential. The boos from the fans unfamiliar with Stoudamire were premature, to say the least, but they served to illustrate just how demanding – and impatient – the Toronto fans might be. To his credit, the young selection didn't pout or get angry. He vowed to prove himself.

"They might have been cheering Ed's name, but by the time I'm finished playing ball, they'll know who Damon Stoudamire is," he said in the moments after his selection.

Second-round draft pick Jimmy King, one of the Fab Five at the University of Michigan, is an impressive leaper whose stock rose in the draft after he was the second leading scorer at the Portland Invitational pre-draft tournament and put in a strong showing at a Chicago pre-draft camp. If he can improve his defence and his perimeter game, he could be a pleasant surprise.

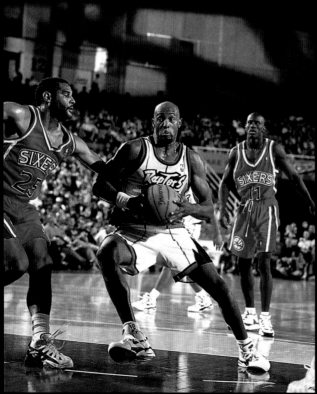

top: *Displaying valuable on-the-floor leadership, Willie Anderson directs his teammates on offence while coach Brendan Malone supervises the activity from the sidelines.* bottom left: *Free-agent Alvin Robertson, a former all NBA defensive team star, brings a decades' experience to the young Raptors.* bottom right: *Robertson, here setting for a three-point attempt adds an offensive threat to his defensive strength.* facing page: *Seizing offensive momentum, Ed Pinckney throws down a power slam against the 76ers.*

TORONTO RAPTORS FOUNDATION

A large measure of social responsibility comes with membership in the NBA, a league which takes its charity work extremely seriously, knowing it and its members must be solid citizens of the community.

Thus comes the Toronto Raptors Foundation, established as a fundraising arm of the team to help worthy causes throughout Toronto, southern Ontario and Canada.

The foundation has already made a substantial mark on the charity landscape in Toronto, making donations and teaming with other organizations to develop programs which benefit not only young basketball players but young Canadians as well. Together with their expansion cousins, the Vancouver Grizzlies, the Raptors are spreading the NBA's Stay in School gospel to Canada's youth.

In August, the Foundation announced donations of $1.3 million to three Ontario-based medical groups to help with funding for cancer and leukemia research, and upgrading of computer facilities at a centre for studies of children at risk. Coming on the heels of a large donation to the Canadian Hemophilia Society as well as a joint venture with Nike to upgrade recreational facilities in Toronto, the Raptors have shown they fit in well with the NBA's desire to help wherever it can.

"Our charity work is extremely important," says team president John Bitove, Jr. "We realize our responsibility to our community."

The foundation has a goal of raising more than $5 million in the first three years of its existence, along with $1 million a year after that. It is administered by a board of directors that includes representatives of the public at large. The stated goal of the Toronto Raptors Foundation is "to support youth programs and other charitable causes province-wide."

Joining Stoudamire and King in the Raptors' locker room will be a host of more experienced players. Leading the team on the court in its premier season will be Toronto's selections from the 1995 NBA expansion draft which was held on June 24.

The expansion draft structure made it virtually impossible for the new teams to get more than a couple of solid NBA players. Existing teams could protect eight players, unrestricted free agents did not have to be protected, and restricted free agents became unrestricted if they were selected, allowing them to make any deal with any team. Thomas and his basketball minds were left with little to choose from. To his credit, Thomas has shown he'll take a chance. With the first pick in the expansion draft he selected Chicago point guard B. J. Armstrong, then upon discovering that Armstrong did not want to play out his career on an expansion team, promptly traded him to the Golden State Warriors in return for five players – Victor Alexander, Carlos Rogers and the Warriors' three second-round draft picks, Dwayne Whitfield, Martin Lewis and Michael McDonald. He also took centre Oliver Miller, whose chronic weight problem cost him jobs with the Phoenix Suns and Detroit Pistons. He took Dontonio Wingfield from the Seattle SuperSonics despite the fact Wingfield left college after just one year and still has plenty of developing to do. He selected John Salley from Miami,

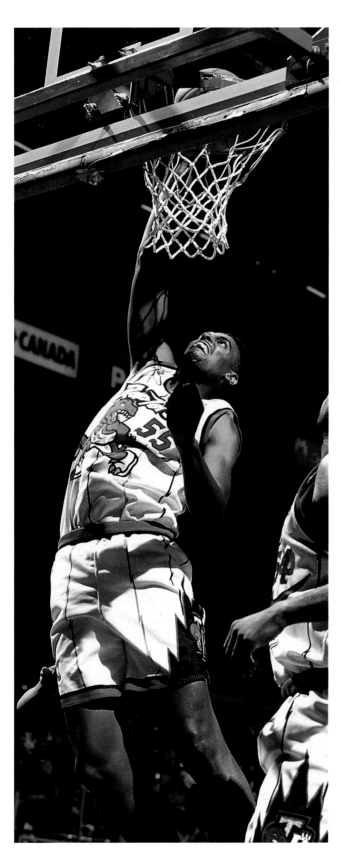

left: *Celtics first-round draft pick in 1993, Raptors centre Acie Earl makes a strong move to the hoop for two against the Grizzlies.* right: *Zan Tabak powers up to the basket with a Philadelphia defender draped on his back.*

left: *Defence is key for any team, but especially for an expansion franchise. Here Ed Pinckney and Willie Anderson close off Grizzlies centre Benoit Benjamin.* **top right:** *Former Pistons starter John Salley rips a rebound against the Grizzlies.* **bottom right:** *Showing no intimidation, six-foot-nine Raptors centre Oliver Miller fires a hook shot over towering seven-foot-six Shawn Bradley of the 76ers.*

an old Pistons teammate of Thomas' who can lend some leadership and levity to the locker room. He took a couple of enigmas in Croatian centre Zan Tabak of the Houston Rockets and Philly guard B. J. Tyler.

He took Jerome Kersey of the Portland Trail Blazers – a pick that was financially astute at least because the Trail Blazers would pay all of Kersey s $4.4 million contract. He signed little-known free agent Vincenzo Esposito to a three-year contract from the Italian professional league, confident that he can adapt to the NBA style of play.

"I think the players we got fit into what we're trying to achieve," Thomas says. "Some of them might not be here when we start playing, and not many of them will be here when we win our first championship. But a lot of them will make a contribution to us in establishing the franchise and what it stands for."

"This is a new beginning for these guys and they should be excited about coming to Toronto," Head Coach Brendan Malone said after the expansion draft. "They're going to find out they are going to get a lot of opportunity to play here."

"The first decision I had to make when I took this job," says Thomas, "is do we want to be a championship team or do we just want to put a good product on the floor? I've always been taught to be the best at what you do, and the best in this league is a championship. That's the path we're going to take. The challenge of my position and the role that I have is to communicate my philosophy to coaches, players, throughout the whole organization, the whole city and the country. I have to make them buy into it and understand what it's about and make everyone see his or her importance in being part of a vision of winning a championship. Each person has to understand how significant they are to reaching that destination."

When the 34-year-old Isiah Lord Thomas III speaks of winning championships, he speaks from a wealth of experience. He was a winner in college at Indiana, where Bobby Knight ruled with an iron fist, and Thomas was able to put his coach's well-defined plan into action. He was a winner in the NBA, guiding the Detroit Pistons to the NBA Finals in 1989 and

far left: *Coach Brendan Malone acts as the catalyst, sparking team chemistry among players new to each other.*
left: *Reunited in a new city, Malone and Salley form part of the strong Detroit Pistons flavour of the Toronto franchise.*

VANCOUVER GRIZZLIES

While there was a competition between three groups to own the NBA's first international expansion franchise in Toronto, for the Vancouver Grizzlies, becoming a reality was just a matter of time.

Vancouver's Arthur Griffiths, chairman of what was then known as Northwest Arena Corp., a subsidiary of Northwest Sports Enterprises which owned the NHL's Vancouver Canucks, was in the process of constructing a brand new, 20,000-seat arena, and the thought of a second major tenant was almost too good to be true.

The Vancouver Mounties – a name which would eventually be cast aside because of trademark difficulties – were quickly born, and the west coast full-court press of the NBA expansion committee began. A meeting with the expansion committee in September 1993 further enhanced the proposition as Jerry Colangelo, the Phoenix Suns owner and committee chairman, came away impressed: "We came into this thing thinking one team, now two is a possibility."

In his drive to bring a second major league team to Vancouver, Griffiths needed an infusion of money to help offset franchise fees, operating costs and the cost of the new General Motors Place, which opened on time and on budget in September 1995. He reached a deal with Seattle businessman John E. McCaw, Jr. which saw a restructuring of Northwest.

Griffiths, as civic-minded an entrepreneur as any city has known, convinced the NBA Vancouver was a perfectly logical extension of its international expansion plans, and on April 27, 1994, the league's board of governors gave its approval to the addition of Vancouver as its 29th franchise. Griffiths has since restructured his empire again, with the McCaw investment truly representing a silent majority, and the newly named corporate entity, Orca Bay Sports & Entertainment, has built an expansion franchise the city, the country and basketball fans everywhere can be proud of.

It also provides a brilliant opportunity to further the spirit of competition which already exists between the two cities. The NHL's Canucks and Maple Leafs fought an intense Stanley Cup semi-final in the spring of 1994, and the CFL's Lions and Argonauts staged a memorable Grey Cup battle in 1983.

1990, doing whatever it took to reach that pinnacle, always focused on that ultimate destination. Thomas was a winner, and he is determined to be a winner again.

"When I came to this job I did some research. I looked at people who win," he recalls of his move from the floor to the front office, a move hastened by a torn Achilles tendon that ended his playing career late in the 1993-94 season. "Winning is not an accident, and that's why the same people win consistently over and over and over again. Talent helps, but talent doesn't drive everything. You look at Tex Schramm and the Dallas Cowboys and what they did, you look at the Raiders and what they did, the Celtics, the Lakers, you look back at the Green Bay Packers. You look just down the road at the Montreal Canadiens and see the way they dominated their sport. That wasn't by accident, and I want to do the same thing with the Raptors that those teams have done. You want to have that type of success, that type of aura.

"You have to lay the foundation in order to build a house, and then you establish the rules in your house, and you don't just let anybody come inside," says Thomas. "There are certain rules you make, certain people you want to attract. They may act some way in some other organization, but we'll do things a little differently around here. We won't be strict disciplinarians

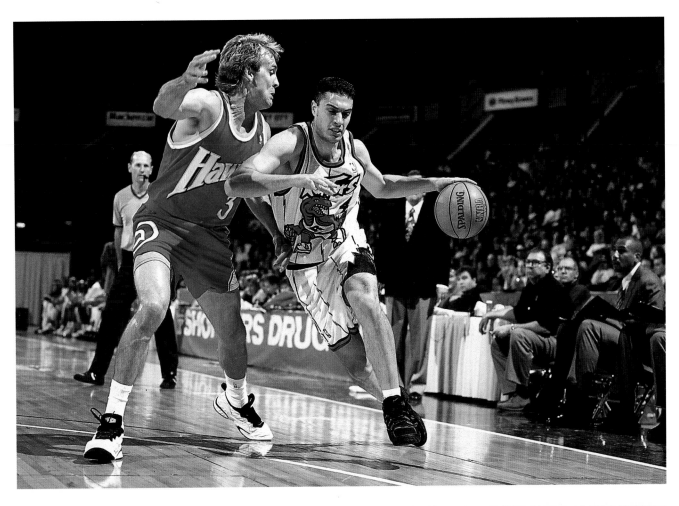

top: *Former Italian league standout Vincenzo Esposito drives around Craig Ehlo of the Atlanta Hawks.* bottom left: *A quick first step and remarkable leaping ability helps Carlos Rogers elude Vernon Maxwell en route to the basket.* bottom right: *Pumped up with enthusiasm, Rogers is a spirited on-court cheerleader for the young Raptors.*

or anything, but there will be such a thing as a Raptors way. And that way will be aimed at winning a championship. From Day One."

Day One, however, had to wait. Just when all eyes were on basketball, just days after the draft had caused such a flurry among the basketball fans of Toronto, the rug was pulled out from under the team by a July 1 lockout.

The lockout, the first work stoppage in league history, caused particular consternation to Thomas, Malone, Scouting Director Bob Zuffelato and the rest of the staff who wanted desperately to see what their roster would look like. A planned free-agent and rookie camp had to be cancelled, a franchise in the New York summer league scrapped. Thomas and his staff were in basketball limbo, anxious to put a team on the floor somewhere but prohibited from even cursory discussions with their players.

However, after two months of inactivity, the league and its players' union came to a contract agreement – a new six-year contract was signed without losing a single minute of regular season action.

The lifting of the lockout allowed Thomas to finally get down to the business of putting the team together that will take the floor for the Raptors' inaugural season. A pre-season victory over Philadelphia in Halifax was an encouraging sign, but the team's brightest moment of their exhibition season came against their expansion cousins in the first-ever Naismith Cup, to be held annually between the Raptors and Grizzlies.

Round 1 of the cross-country court war went to the Raptors in what became a celebration of basketball in Canada. Toronto scored a 98-77 victory as 11,203 fans at the Winnipeg Arena witnessed history.

For as long as the Canadian franchises exist, any meeting between the teams will be important for fans across Canada. For the Raptors, their victory holds the promise of a bright future for an exciting new edition to the NBA galaxy.

From a seed planted in John Bitove's mind, those years ago when he watched a young Isiah Thomas stride the Indiana hardwood, has grown an historic franchise, with strong roots in its nation's premier city. With the powerful combination of the two men's business sense and basketball savvy, Toronto fans can be confident they will soon reap the harvest of NBA success.

R a p t o r s   p l a y e r   p r o f i l e s

The Toronto Raptors launched their inaugural pre-season campaign featuring the players listed on these pages.

ED PINCKNEY – FORWARD

Six foot nine
240 lbs.
Milwaukee Bucks
March 27, 1963
10 years in NBA

Team	G	FGM	FGA	PCT	FTM	FTA	PCT	REBS	AST	BLK	PPG
85-94 Pho/Sac/Bos	630	1673	3102	.539	1348	1758	.767	3218	628	381	7.5
94-95 Milwaukee	62	48	97	.495	44	62	.710	211	21	17	2.3
Career	692	1721	3199	.538	1392	1820	.757	3429	649	398	7.0
Career Playoffs	28	60	98	.612	52	63	.825	135	10	12	6.1

WILLIE ANDERSON – GUARD

Six foot eight
200 lbs.
San Antonio Spurs
January 8, 1967
Seven years in NBA

TEAM	G	FGM	FGA	PCT	3-PT	FG	PCT	FTM	FTA	PCT	REBS	AST	PPG
88-94 San Antonio	413	2411	5066	.476	54	214	.252	885	1129	.784	1739	1822	13.9
94-95 San Antonio	38	76	162	.469	3	19	.158	30	41	.732	55	52	4.9
Career	451	2487	5228	.476	57	233	.245	915	1170	.782	1794	1874	13.2
94-95 Playoffs	11	9	20	.450	0	1	.000	2	3	.667	12	10	1.8
Career Playoffs	39	180	375	.480	11	28	.393	58	76	.763	116	121	11.2

ACIE EARL – CENTRE

Six foot 10
240 lbs
Boston Celtics
June 23, 1970
Two years in NBA

TEAM	G	FGM	FGA	PCT	FTM	FTA	PCT	REBS	AST	BLK	PPG
93-94 Boston	74	151	372	.406	108	160	.675	247	12	53	5.5
94-95 Boston	30	26	68	.382	14	29	.483	45	2	8	2.2
Career	104	177	440	.402	122	189	.645	292	14	61	4.6
94-95 Playoffs	1	1	3	.333	0	2	.000	2	0	1	2.0

ZAN TABAK – CENTRE

Seven feet
245 lbs.
Houston Rockets
June 15, 1970
One year in NBA

TEAM	G	FGM	FGA	PCT	FTM	FTA	PCT	REBS	AST	BLK	PPG
94-95 Houston	37	24	53	.453	27	44	.614	57	4	7	2.0
94-95 Playoffs	8	2	5	.400	2	2	1.000	1	1	3	0.8

B.J. TYLER – GUARD

Six foot one
185 lbs.
Philadelphia 76ers
April 30, 1971
One year in NBA

TEAM	G	FGM	FGA	PCT	3-PT	FG	PCT	FTM	FTA	PCT	REBS	AST	PPG
94-95 Philadelphia	55	72	189	.381	16	51	.314	35	50	.700	62	174	3.5

VICTOR ALEXANDER – CENTRE/FORWARD*

Six foot 10
265 lbs.
Golden State Warriors
August 31, 1969
Four years in NBA

TEAM	G	FGM	FGA	PCT	3-PT	FG	PCT	FTM	FTA	PCT	REBS	AST	PPG
91-94 Golden State	221	853	1628	.524	12	36	.333	282	440	.641	1064	191	9.1
94-95 Golden State	50	230	447	.515	6	25	.240	36	60	.600	291	60	10.0
Career	271	1083	2075	.522	18	61	.295	318	500	.636	1355	251	9.2
Career Playoffs	4	3	5	.600	0	0	.000	1	1	1.000	6	1	1.8

JOHN SALLEY – FORWARD/CENTRE

Six foot 11
255 lbs.
Miami Heat
May 16, 1964
Nine years in NBA

TEAM	G	FGM	FGA	PCT	FTM	FTA	PCT	REBS	AST	BLK	PPG
86-94 Det/Mia	586	1586	3093	.513	1250	1756	.712	2815	713	857	7.6
94-95 Miami	75	197	395	.499	153	207	.739	336	123	85	7.3
Career	661	1783	3488	.511	1403	1963	.715	3151	836	942	7.5
Career Playoffs	100	285	562	.507	256	367	.698	555	94	151	8.3

OLIVER MILLER – CENTRE

Six foot nine
280 lbs.
Detroit Pistons
April 6, 1970
Three years in NBA

TEAM	G	FGM	FGA	PCT	FTM	FTA	PCT	REBS	AST	BLK	PPG
92-94 Phoenix	125	398	710	.561	151	237	.637	751	362	256	7.6
94-95 Detroit	64	232	418	.555	78	124	.629	475	93	116	8.5
Career	189	630	1128	.559	229	361	.634	1226	455	372	7.9
Career Playoffs	34	87	148	.588	34	62	.548	168	64	71	6.1

ANDRES GUIBERT – FORWARD

Six foot 10
242 lbs.
Minnesota Timberwolves
October 28, 1968
Two years in NBA

TEAM	G	FGM	FGA	PCT	FTM	FTA	PCT	REBS	AST	BLK	PPG
93-94 Minnesota	5	6	20	.300	3	6	.500	16	2	1	3.0
94-95 Minnesota	17	16	47	.340	13	19	.684	45	10	1	2.6
Career	22	22	67	.328	16	25	.640	61	12	2	2.7

TONY MASSENBURG – FORWARD

Six foot nine
245 lbs.
Los Angeles Clippers
July 31, 1967
Three years in NBA

TEAM	G	FGM	FGA	PCT	FTM	FTA	PCT	REBS	AST	BLK	PPG
90-92 S.A./Cha/ Bos/G.S.	53	37	85	.435	37	60	.617	83	4	10	2.1
92-94 Italian League											
94-95 L.A. Clippers	80	282	601	.469	177	235	.753	455	67	58	9.3
Career	133	319	686	.465	214	295	.725	538	71	68	6.4
Career Playoffs	1	0	0	.000	0	0	.000	0	0	0	0.0

CARLOS ROGERS – FORWARD/CENTRE*

Six foot 11
220 lbs.
Golden State Warriors
February 6, 1971
One year in NBA

TEAM	G	FGM	FGA	PCT	3-PT	FG	PCT	FTM	FTA	PCT	REBS	AST	PPG
94-95 Golden State	49	180	340	.529	2	14	.143	76	146	.521	278	37	8.9

ROOKIES

DAMON STOUDAMIRE – GUARD

First round,
* seventh overall*
Five foot 10
171 lbs.
Arizona
September 3, 1973

TEAM	G	FGM	FGA	PCT	3-PT	FG	PCT	FTM	FTA	PCT	REBS	AST	PPG
91-92 Arizona	30	76	167	.455	28	69	.406	37	48	.771	65	76	7.2
92-93 Arizona	28	99	226	.438	39	102	.382	72	91	.791	116	159	11.0
93-94 Arizona	35	217	484	.448	93	265	.351	112	140	.800	157	208	18.3
94-95 Arizona	30	222	466	.476	112	241	.465	128	155	.826	128	220	22.8
Career	123	614	1343	.457	272	677	.402	349	434	.804	466	663	15.0

JIMMY KING – GUARD

Second round,
* 35th overall*
Six foot five
210 lbs.
Michigan
August 9, 1973

TEAM	G	FGM	FGA	PCT	3-PT	FG	PCT	FTM	FTA	PCT	REBS	AST	PPG
91-92 Michigan	34	128	258	.496	28	60	.467	53	72	.736	112	78	9.9
92-93 Michigan	36	148	291	.509	37	92	.402	57	88	.648	159	110	10.8
93-94 Michigan	29	139	284	.489	29	87	.333	51	79	.646	109	76	12.3
94-95 Michigan	31	168	388	.478	28	109	.257	93	137	.679	155	90	14.7
Career	130	583	1221	.477	122	348	.350	254	376	.675	535	354	11.9

DWAYNE WHITFIELD – FORWARD*

Second round,
* 40th overall by*
* Golden State Warriors*
Six foot nine, 240 lbs.
Jackson State
August 21, 1972

TEAM	G	FGM	FGA	PCT	3-PT	FG	PCT	FTM	FTA	PCT	REBS	AST	PPG
92-93 JSU	12	29	60	.483	0	0	.000	15	26	.577	46	2	6.1
93-94 JSU	29	136	237	.574	0	1	.000	88	123	.715	195	17	12.4
94-95 JSU	26	194	318	.610	0	3	.000	121	195	.621	273	15	19.6
Career	67	359	615	.584	0	4	.000	224	344	.651	514	34	14.1

VINCENZO ESPOSITO – GUARD

Six foot three
198 lbs.
Free Agent
Italian League
March 1, 1969

TEAM	G	FGM	FGA	PCT	3-PT	FG	PCT	FTM	FTA	PCT	REBS	AST	PPG
84-85 Caserta	5	1	1	1.000	0	0	.000	2	3	.667	0	1	0.8
85-87 Caserta	71	62	128	.484	12	32	.375	35	45	.777	28	26	2.2
87-89 Caserta	68	241	471	.512	53	149	.356	132	153	.863	122	60	9.7
89-93 Caserta	143	811	1723	.471	255	666	.383	463	550	.842	275	131	16.1
93-94 Bologna	30	219	557	.393	74	239	.310	207	248	.835	55	52	24.0
94-95 Bologna	31	217	488	.444	95	245	.388	221	238	.929	53	59	24.2
Career	348	1551	3368	.461	489	1331	.367	1060	1237	.857	533	329	13.4

MARTIN LEWIS – GUARD*

Second round,
* 50th overall by*
* Golden State Warriors*
Six foot six, 225 lbs.
Seward CC
April 28, 1975

TEAM	G	FGM	FGA	PCT	3-PT	FG	PCT	FTM	FTA	PCT	REBS	AST	PPG
93-94 But	29	188	342	.550	0	0	.000	94	145	.648	177	0	17.6
94-95 Scw	37	307	472	.650	22	78	.282	202	307	.658	304	64	22.6
Career	66	495	814	.608	22	78	.282	296	452	.655	481	64	20.4

*Acquired through trade of B.J. Armstrong to Golden State.

1 9 9 5 - 9 6 schedule

N O V E M B E R

3	New Jersey	9:00 p.m.
4	Indiana	7:30 p.m.
7	Chicago	8:30 p.m.
8	Sacramento	7:00 p.m.
10	Phoenix	7:00 p.m.
11	Charlotte	7:30 p.m.
13	Utah	7:00 p.m.
15	Houston	7:00 p.m.
17	Minnesota	7:00 p.m.
18	Washington	7:30 p.m.
21	Seattle	8:00 p.m.
22	Milwaukee	8:30 p.m.
25	Atlanta	7:30 p.m.
27	Golden State	7:00 p.m.
28	Cleveland	7:30 p.m.

D E C E M B E R

1	Philadelphia	7:00 p.m.
3	Miami	5:30 p.m.
5	Seattle	10:00 p.m.
7	Portland	10:00 p.m.
8	L.A. Lakers	10:30 p.m.
10	Vancouver	8:30 p.m.
12	Boston	7:00 p.m.
14	Indiana	7:00 p.m.
15	Boston	7:30 p.m.
17	Orlando	5:30 p.m.
19	Detroit	7:00 p.m.
22	Chicago	8:30 p.m.
23	New York	7:30 p.m.
26	vs. Milwaukee at Hamilton	1:30 p.m.
28	Detroit	7:30 p.m.

J A N U A R Y

3	Orlando	7:30 p.m.
4	Atlanta	7:30 p.m.
9	Charlotte	7:00 p.m.
11	Atlanta	7:00 p.m.
13	Washington	6:00 p.m.
15	New Jersey	7:30 p.m.
16	Indiana	7:00 p.m.
18	Chicago	7:00 p.m.
21	Boston	noon
23	New Jersey	7:00 p.m.
25	Vancouver	8:30 p.m.
27	Denver	9:00 p.m.
30	Sacramento	10:30 p.m.

F E B R U A R Y

2	Golden State	10:30 p.m.
3	L.A. Clippers	10:30 p.m.
5	Portland	7:00 p.m.
7	Milwaukee	7:00 p.m.
13	Miami	7:30 p.m.
15	vs. Cleveland at Hamilton	7:00 p.m.
17	Detroit	7:30 p.m.
22	Utah	9:00 p.m.
23	Phoenix	9:00 p.m.
25	Dallas	8:00 p.m.
27	Houston	8:30 p.m.
29	San Antonio	8:30 p.m.

M A R C H

3	Cleveland	3:00 p.m.
5	Detroit	7:00 p.m.
6	New York	7:00 p.m.
8	Miami	7:30 p.m.
10	Dallas	8:00 p.m.
12	Philadelphia	7:30 p.m.
15	Charlotte	7:30 p.m.
17	Indiana	3:00 p.m.
18	Denver	7:00 p.m.
20	Charlotte	7:00 p.m.
22	San Antonio	7:00 p.m.
24	Chicago	3:30 p.m.
26	Atlanta	7:00 p.m.
27	Philadelphia	7:30 p.m.
29	Orlando	7:00 p.m.
31	L.A. Lakers	3:00 p.m.

A P R I L

2	L.A. Clippers	7:00 p.m.
4	Cleveland	7:00 p.m.
6	New York	6:00 p.m.
8	Minnesota	8:00 p.m.
9	Milwaukee	8:30 p.m.
12	Boston	7:30 p.m.
14	Washington	1:00 p.m.
15	New York	7:30 p.m.
17	New Jersey	7:30 p.m.
19	Washington	7:00 p.m.
21	Philadelphia	1:00 p.m.

All Times EST

■ Home games

■ Away games

a c k n o w l e d g e m e n t s

Opus Productions Inc.

President/Creative Director: Derik Murray   Vice President/Publishing Director: Marthe Love
Vice President, Production: David Counsell   Chief Financial Officer: Jamie Engen
Design/Electronic Art: Guylaine Rondeau   Legal Counsel: John Nicolls
Electronic Art: Paul Despins   Project/Editorial Coordinator: Wendy Darling
Visual Coordinator: Joanne Powers   Editor: Brian Scrivener
Design Consultant: Jeff McLean   Assistant Editorial Coordinator: Michelle Hunter

Marketing Manager: David Attard
Marketing Consultant: Glenn McPherson

Opus Productions would like to thank the management and staff of the Toronto Raptors Basketball Club Inc., especially the following:

John Bitove, Jr., President
Isiah Thomas, Executive Vice President, Basketball Operations
John Lashway, Executive Director, Communications
Elaine McKeracher, Manager, Media Relations
Matt Akler, Media Relations Assistant
George Borges, Consumer Product Division
Sandy Romas, Executive Assistant to the President
Jessica Guyor, Executive Assistant to Isiah Thomas
Stephanie Jamieson, Manager, Ticket Office
Susan MacIver, Administrative Assistant, Stadium, Air Canada Centre

Opus Productions appreciates the generous assistance and support of the National Basketball Association, and extends special thanks to:

National Basketball Association Properties, Inc.
Frank Fochetta, Director and Group Manager, NBA Publishing
Diane Naughton, Director of Publishing

National Basketball Association Entertainment, Inc.
Carmin Romanelli, Manager, NBA Photos
Joe Amati, Photo Assistant
Eric Weinstein, Photo Assistant

National Basketball Association Communications Group
Alex Sachare, Vice President, Editorial
Mark Broussard, Staff Writer

Opus Productions is grateful to the following individuals and institutions for their assistance and support:

Dr. James Naismith Basketball Foundation   Naismith Memorial Basketball Hall of Fame
Almonte, Ontario   Springfield, Massachusetts
John Gosset   Wayne Patterson

Ken Allen, Evan Hargreaves, Nike Canada • Kate Bowden, Becky Lloyd-Scalco, Nike Inc. • Michael Burch, Nick Rundall, Whitecap Books Limited • Brian Cooper Nancy Dodd, Rackets and Runners • Jerry Eberts • Robin Evans • Linda Goodman, Don Ogden, Supreme Graphics • Diane Grant • Mary Hermant • Steve McKinnon, City of Toronto Archives • Melinda Misener • David Schmidt, Spalding Canada • David Strickland • Cathy Valenti, Logo Athletic (A Division of N.T.D.) • Allie Wilmink

Author's Note

There are several people without whose assistance this book would not have been possible. I would like to thank my wife Susan Walsh, whose patience, understanding and support were never ending and who made many sacrifices for which I am forever grateful. I would also like to thank John Bitove and Isiah Thomas for their time and valuable insight into the birth of the franchise and the building of a team. Also deserving are my bosses and co-workers at The Canadian Press.
DOUG SMITH

Photo Credits

Courtesy of **Air Canada Centre**: 16; **Baptist, Bill**/NBA Photos: 108 2nd from top, 4th from top; **Bénard, Joël**: 8; **Bernstein, Andrew D.**/NBA Photos: 17, 32 left, 33, 34, 35 right, 36-37, 40 left, 45 left, 50, 51 bottom left, 54-55, 62 top left, 68-69, 71 right, 80 right, 83 right, 86 bottom, 41 bottom right; **Bettmann/UPI**: 28, 29 left & right, 30 left & right, 31; **Butler, Nathaniel S.**/NBA Photos: 15 left, 35 left, 39, 40 right, 44, 48 left, 53, 57 bottom, 59, 63 right, 66 left, 73 top right, 76, 78-79 top & bottom, 80 left, 81 top & bottom, 82 left & right, 83 top left, 84, 87, 88, 92 right, 93, 94 top & bottom, 95 top left, bottom left, top right & bottom right, 96 left &

right, 97 left, 98 top, bottom left & bottom right, 99, 101 left & right, 102 bottom right, 103 left & right, 105 top, bottom left & bottom right, 106 left & right; **Capozzola, Lou**/NBA Photos: 77 left, 85, 108 3rd from top, 4th from bottom; Courtesy of **City of Toronto Archives, Globe & Mail Collection**: 27 top #110886 & bottom #110884; **Cole, Barbara**: 4; **Covatta, Chris**/NBA Photos: 108 3rd from bottom; **Cunningham, Scott**/NBA Photos: 3, 41 bottom left, 46-47, 48 left, 56, 62 bottom left, 73 bottom left, 74 right, 75 right, 83 bottom left; **Defrisco, Tim**/Allsport: 52 right, 62 bottom right; **Defrisco, Tim**/NBA Photos: 58 left, 64 right, 109 top;

Drake, Brian/NBA Photos: 57 top; **Forencich, Sam**/NBA Photos: 71 left, 73 left, 109 3rd from top; **Forwerck, Gregg**/NBA Photos: 108 bottom; **Gossage, Barry**/NBA Photos: 45 right, 49, 66 top right, 67, 77 right; **Hayt, Andy**/NBA Photos: 62 top right, 63 left, 64 left, 70, 74 left, 86 top left & top right; **Hayt, Ron**/NBA Photos: 102 left & top right, 107; **Hoskins, Ron**/NBA Photos: 95, 109 4th from bottom; **James, Glenn**/NBA Photos: 72; **Lewis, Richard**/NBA Photo: 108 2nd from bottom; **McElligott, William**: 18, 22 left & right, 24-25; **Millan, Manny**/Sports Illustrated: 51 top, 58 right; **Murdoch, Layne**/NBA Photos: 66 bottom right; Courtesy of **Naismith**

Foundation, Almonte, Ont.: 23; **NBA Photo Library**: 10 bottom; Courtesy of **Naismith Memorial Basketball Hall of Fame**: 19, 20 top & bottom, 21, 26; **Sierra, Hector**/NBA Photos: 52 left; **Schwartzman, Bruce L.**: 109 4th from top Soohoo, Jon/NBA Photos: 14, 32 right; **Stroud, Jason**/Derik Murray Photography Inc.: 6, 12, 38, 60-61, 89, 90, 100; **Trotman, Noren**/NBA Photos: 41 top, 51 bottom right, 65, 108 top; Courtesy of **Turenne, Ron**/Toronto Raptors: 10 top, 11, 12, 13 top left, top right & bottom left, bottom right, 15 right, 92 left, 97 right; **Widner, Rocky**/NBA Photos: 9, 75 left, 109 2nd from top.

Hoops comes home!
Get inside the action with this complete guide to basketball and the NBA.

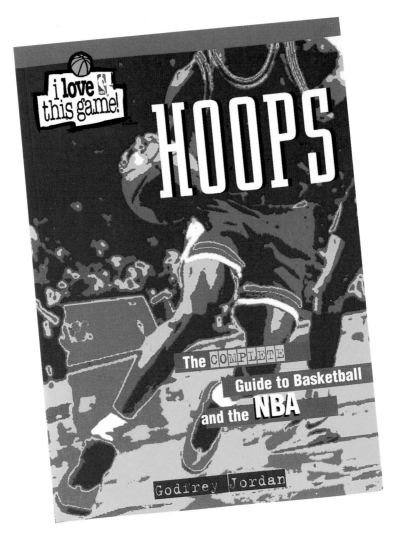

Since its creation in 1891 by a young Canadian, Dr. James Naismith, basketball has been a part of our national sports scene in schools and local leagues. Did you know the NBA's very first game was played at Maple Leaf Gardens in 1946 with the Toronto Huskies up against the New York Knicks!

Hoops! shows you the game's evolution, the basic rules, player positions, strategies and little-known highlights of hoop history. You'll learn how to translate the box scores and stay informed with a complete dictionary of basketball terms and a team directory.

Fully endorsed by the NBA, *Hoops!* is illustrated throughout and includes a colour photo section, charts and stats. A must for every fan – young and old – *Hoops!* is your fast break to follow all the action.

Now available in bookstores everywhere.